THE
END GAME

DICK ROTHSCHILD

D1403494

By the same author –
  Better Health, simple sensible strategies

THE END GAME
by
Dick Rothschild

Copyright © Dick Rothschild. 2019
Cover Copyright © Kitty Honeycutt (Ravenswood Publishing)
Published by Sly Fox
(An Imprint of Ravenswood Publishing)

Ravenswood Publishing
1275 Baptist Chapel Rd.
Autryville, NC 28318
http://www.ravenswoodpublishing.com
Email: RavenswoodPublishing@gmail.com

Paperback orders can be placed through Amazon
http://www.amazon.com

Printed in the United States of America
First Edition
10 9 8 7 6 5 4 3 2 1

ISBN-13: 978-0-578-53457-2

Acknowledgement

I am not a fan of the overreaching acknowledgement which heaps thanks on every breathing body with whom the author has been in contact during the writing process. If all those individuals actually had their fingers in the literary pie, it would never have made it out of the oven.

Thanks where thanks are due. This novella might not have been accepted by two publishers had it not been for the input of two consummate professionals. Stacey Donovan provided the insightful evaluation and critique of the first draft. Further along, Don White followed with a masterful developmental copy and line edit. I am profoundly grateful to them both.

For Olga, the love of my life

"Life shrinks or expands in proportion to one's courage."

—Anais Nin

CHAPTER ONE

"No time for second thoughts," big Bob Rosenbaum says to himself as he hesitatingly allows a nurse to help him onto the gurney. "Just suck it up." Bob senses that the gurney is rolling. and a blur of creamy ceiling panels, glaring fluorescent lights, and bronzed door frames slide by. As the gurney stops momentarily, the hiss of pneumatic doors masks his erratic heartbeat but not his apprehensiveness. His wife, Hildy has been dead for just three months and now he is being wheeled into surgery for a procedure to normalize his heartbeat and improve his breathing. The gurney rolls on, stops under a battery of silvery reflector lights. Blue-clad technicians spring into motion, execute deft movements while they ask rehearsed questions, like veteran theatrical performers. "Your date of birth?" "Do you know what procedure you're here for?" "Are you warm enough?" And, as actors might, in the prologue of a stage play, each steps into the spotlight, briefly explains his or her role in the forthcoming drama, and then withdraws to make room for the next.

Two burly assistants slide him off the gurney onto the operating table. Then a youthful intern straps him down. Bob eyes the intern apprehensively, as the image of a convicted criminal being strapped down on an execution table flashes before his mind. Has his courage to confront adversity, on which he has prided himself, he wonders, suddenly abandoned him?

"For your safety," explains the intern. "We don't want you to slide off the table and hurt yourself, now, do we?"

"Don't let this kid rattle you", Bob tries to reassure himself. "He's just a supercilious asshole."

Big Bob feels cold wet sensors being pressed against his chest, arms, legs, and hears clicks as they are snapped into spaghetti-like bundles of white, plastic-covered wires leading to a heart monitor. Then, he detects a faint antiseptic odor and feels sharp pricks as they insert IV needles in his wrist and arms.

A white-uniformed cast member approaches, affecting a well-rehearsed smile.

"I'm Dr. Wang. I will be your anesthesiologist for this procedure."

"Can you hear me Mr. Rosenberg?"

"Loud and clear -- and the name's, Rosenbaum."

"Sorry, Mr. Ro-zen-baum. Now, I'm going to give you something to help you relax, and just before Dr. Rogers arrives I'll introduce the anesthesia to sedate you during the procedure."

"Do you have any questions?"

"Yeah. Will I be awake? Will I feel pain?"

"So, you may be awake briefly at the beginning of the procedure, but you should not feel any pain. Most patients don't remember anything about it afterwards. So just relax" suggests the anesthesiologist as he too withdraws.

Bob, realizing how difficult it is for him to try to relax under these circumstances, wonders how relaxed the anesthesiologist would be if their positions were reversed.

Then his thoughts take him back to the series of events that led up to his being in the Cardiology Operating Room at Brigham & Women's Hospital, just a month shy of his seventy-ninth birthday.

On a Monday in June, three months earlier, his wife, Hildy, had planned to drive to Boston with her friend Liv Valente to see the new show of contemporary weavings at the MFA.

But, at eight that morning, Liv phoned explaining that she had developed a sore throat and fever and was backing out. Despite having had a sleepless night herself, Hildy decided to drive to Boston on her own to see the museum show.

By June Bob has already begun to experience breathlessness and the irregular heartbeat which had dogged him since then.

Shortly after Hildy had left for Boston, he has taken friends for a sail on his little cat boat, *El Gato*. Late in the morning, after the sail, he settles into a deck chair and is starting to read David Brooks' column in the Times when a patrol car pulls up to the house. Two State troopers get out and clang the nautical bell at the front door. As he opens it, Bob deduces at once, from their unsmiling faces, that this is not going to be a request for a donation to the State Troopers Benevolent Association.

"Mr. Rosenbaum?" asks the senior trooper. Bob nods affirmatively.

"Related to Hildegard"

"My wife."

"I'm afraid I've got some bad news, sir–can we come in?"

Bob, suddenly seized with panic, gasps for breath. All he can manage is to wave them in. The older trooper removes his felt sombrero, the younger nervously follows suit. When Bob feels he can breathe again he asks,

"So, what is it?"

"Maybe you should sit down, sir." Bob, feeling a little unsteady, makes his way over to the dining table and eases himself into one of the Alto side chairs, motions the troopers into others. He is aware that he is perspiring.

"Your wife was in a bad automobile accident - on Route Three."

Bob starts trembling.

"How bad? What happened? Was she hurt? Is she o.k?" The trooper bows his head,

"I'm afraid she didn't make it, sir."

4

"Oh God, no. You mean she's...she's dead?"

"Yes sir."

"No, no. That…that can't be." Bob writhes as if in intense pain and then slowly slumps onto the table, shaking his head and pounding the table with his fist again and again.

"Are you O.K., sir?" the senor trooper rises and bends over him.

"Joe, get Mr. Rosenbaum a glass of water." Bob sits up, reaches for the glass the younger trooper has placed before him, takes a sip, and looks ahead, overwhelmed, too upset to process the information. Then he takes another sip, puts the glass down.

"Are you sure she is dead? What happened?"

"Her car went off the road, on Route Three between exit twelve and thirteen, ran into a tree. We estimate the vehicle was traveling at sixty-five to seventy miles an hour. She was killed instantly. An ambulance took her to Jordan Hospital, where she was declared D.O.A." Bob begins trembling again, his voice now reduced to a croak.

"How is that possible?" "Hildy— she's, she's such a good driver."

"The report says there were no other vehicles involved, so it might have been a heart attack - or she could have fallen asleep and veered off the highway. "

"Where is she now?" The trooper swallows.

"They're holding the body at Jordan, at the hospital, until they hear from a family member."

"The car was totaled. Towed to police headquarters in Hanson. You can contact Sargent Wisnowski at the desk there. I'll write down the phone number and address for you. A complete accident report is being filed and a copy will be available in Hanson tomorrow. When you're feeling up to it, you'll need to contact your insurance agent. Is there someone you'd like us to call to come over now and be with you, sir?" Bob feels exhausted, frightened, abandoned. He senses that he needs to calm himself, to come to grips with the unthinkable situation into which he has been thrust before receiving the attention of well-meaning relatives and friends.

"No, no I just need to be alone - for a while," he says. "When I pull myself together I'll contact the hospital, call my kids, and Lana and Jim, Marion & Bill, a few others. For now, I'll be O.K.," he says.

"Well then, sir, we'll be going along. Here's my card in case you need to contact me. Again, our regrets, sir. Take care of yourself."

Bob covers his eyes. Moments in his life with Hildy parade before him.

He reflects on his relationship with Hildy, the passionate physical attraction slowly metamorphosing into a stimulating and comfortable companionship. His world. His life. Not without scuffles and occasional brawls, both being strong minded and, at times, unyielding. Yet, without Hildy, without her reassuring support, her steadying influence, can he muster the strength and courage to go on? A movement near him reminds Bob that he is the hospital on the operating room table, awaiting an ablation procedure to correct his irregular heartbeat.

The voice of Doctor Wang, the anesthesiologist, penetrates his swirl of thoughts.

"How are you feeling?" asks Wang.

"O.K." I guess," replies Bob

"Dr. Rogers has been delayed, briefly. We've just heard that he is on his way now, so I'm going to start you on the anesthesia. You may start to feel a little drowsy."

The anesthesiologist articulates Rogers's name with reverence. William Bradford Rogers, MD. A star at Tulane Medical School, standout during his residency and fellowship at UCLA, he is now the leading cardiologist at Brigham and Women's. Rogers as he sweeps into the room commands "Stop everything!" then leans over Bob. "Mr. Rosenbaum. Its Doctor Rogers. Can you hear me?"

"Yes"

"At a last-minute check of your CAT scan images we discovered something we hadn't observed before and, we suspect, could be the cause of your irregular heartbeat and breathlessness which would not be corrected by the planned catheter ablation procedure.

"What?"

"It's called amyloidosis, a deposit of protein on the heart wall."

"Serious?"

"Well, it could be, but I'm not a specialist in it. I want you to make an appointment with Henry Hawk. He's the leading specialist in amyloidosis. I'm sending all your records, the blood tests and images, to him, and I'm confident Henry will get to the bottom of it." Rogers pauses for a moment, then adds, "Bob, I am sorry to have put you through all this. I will stay in close touch with Dr. Hawk. Good luck." Bob is momentarily reassured but as soon as Rogerson leaves he is clutched with feelings of self-doubt and guilt tied to long past, stressfully debilitating experiences, his first wife's descent into alcoholism and mental derangement and the death of two sons, Andrew and Carl. He is still haunted by the thought that he could have foreseen and, possibly, somehow prevented these tragedies.

CHAPTER TWO

The next morning Bob phones Dr. Hawk's office and learns that they have yet to receive the medical information from Rogers. They'll call Bob back in a couple of days. He grimaces,

Already unhinged by Rogers' sudden abortion of the catheter ablation, a surgical procedure to normalize his heartbeat and relieve his breathlessness, and anxious about the delay, Bob senses his heart palpitating, his throat tightening and a feeling of helplessness washing over him. Trying to reassert some measure of control, he goes online to learn more about his condition, on his own.

On one website he learns that cardiac amyloidosis is the hardening of the heart wall caused by the deposit of insoluble proteins carried in the blood stream and, more alarmingly, it compromises heart function. On another site he discovers that it is "a very rare disorder that occurs in only one or two people in a million." Bob is aware, now, that his heart is firing like a machine gun. "Don't be a baby," he tells himself as he begins breathing in

9

through his nose and out through his mouth, an exercise his friend Flash has told him, slows down the pulse. Just as it does, he reads that because the disease is so rare, research has not yet discovered a cure for amyloidosis. Apparently, protein just builds up in the heart wall, displacing heart muscle until heart failure occurs. His thoughts toggle between feeling overwhelmed, emotionally wrecked and

desperately wanting to disbelieve this information.

The only potential fix cited is a heart transplant. At the age of seventy-nine, Bob instinctively senses that he is not a good heart transplant candidate.

Bob suddenly feels helpless, as though he has just received a personal death sentence. He grasps at straws. *Maybe I don't have amyloidosis at all, or if I do it could be a disease which, like prostate cancer, develops so slowly in older men that most die of natural causes long before the cancer can do them in.* But then, digging further, Bob is aghast to find out that life expectancy without treatment averages thirteen months—and, with treatment, seventeen months.

Just then his phone rings and the screen shows that the caller is his friend Larry "Flash" Peters.

"Hey, Flash, what's up?" Bob tries to sound upbeat to conceal the distress he is feeling.

"Not much, Rosy. Just wanted to find out how your ablation went."

"It didn't".

"Wha-da-ya-mean?"

"They didn't do it."

"Holy shit, why not?"

"Rogers, the surgeon – at the last minute he thought he saw something new on my CAT scan that could have been causing my irregular heartbeat and breathlessness and figured the ablation wouldn't fix them. He's referred me to a specialist, big honcho cardiologist, name of Hawk." Bob instantly regretted letting the name of the cardiologist slip out. If Flash became curious, he'd easily find out that Hawk was an amyloidosis specialist. No need to upset his friend prematurely.

"I'm waiting to see him. And, I've got to tell you, he is harder to get an appointment with than to get one with George W. when he's watching a Texas Rangers game"

"So, in the meantime, they've just got you hanging, Rosy? That sucks."

"Yeah, it sucks." Bob says in only a slightly disparaging tone, trying to spare his friend from the anger welling up in him for having been put off so long for the appointment.

"So, how are you feeling?"

"Fine, the ticker is behaving itself, at least for the moment," he fibs.

"Coming to tennis on Tuesday?"

"Wouldn't miss it." He says reassuringly, though he's thinking that he would just as soon pass it up.

"See you there. Oh, and be sure to let me know if you hear from this Hawk character." Bob winces. The amyloidosis specialist's name hasn't escaped Flash Peters.

CHAPTER THREE

Each day that he doesn't hear back from Hawk's office depletes his spirits further until by the fourth day he feels so drained that he finds himself struggling just to get out of bed in the morning. Bob realizes he can wait no longer and calls again.

"Have you received the information from Dr. Rogerson?" A brief silence follows.

"Yes, we've got it. Did you want to make an appointment with Dr. Hawk?" *For God's sake', Bob thinks, here I am, my life hanging in the balance on what this quack has to say, and she wants to know if I want to make an appointment with him.'*

"Yes, I want an appointment – as soon as possible," he replies testily.

"The earliest opening, I have for Dr. Hawk is next month on November twenty-first."

"Can't you get me in sooner?" Another pause. He feels as though he is hanging from a rope which could break at any moment ending his life.

"Dr. Hawk only sees patients on Fridays, after his surgeries.

Can you come in at 5 PM on Friday, November Seventh?"

"I can." He feels some relief.

"You'll need to get here an hour early for an echocardiogram– Dr. Hawk will want to look at it before seeing you.

"An echocardiogram? I just had an echocardiogram, a couple of weeks ago at Brigham and Women's, in preparation for the procedure that Dr. Rogerson was planning to do. Won't that do?" he says, unable to conceal his irritation

"Hold the phone a minute? I'll find out." The phone goes silent for a minute and a half.

"Sorry to keep you waiting. No, Doctor wants to see an echocardiogram on the day you come in - so plan to arrive at four PM. You'll receive instructions and directions to the Imaging Center the Shapiro Building in a few days by email. Let me have your email address and phone number."

The next three weeks Bob finds himself on an emotional rollercoaster, first climbing up and sensing a certain relief at getting closer to an answer about his condition, then plunging down into despair that the answer he is about to get will be devastating. If only

Hildy were here to calm and comfort him as she had when his mother had suffered a heart attack.

The best of times for Bob are those in which he can distract himself. Flirting indifferently with lithesome Lisa at the front desk at the Forever Fit Gym–December's inconsequential pursuit of June; writing his next column for The Schooner; playing tennis with Flash, Jean, and Jim, having drinks and dinner with Liv and Peter or Squeaky and Sam, or practicing his guitar. All serve as temporary defenses, keeping AMYLOIDOSIS, the elephant in the room, at

bay. But, if he's waiting in line at the Stop and Shop checkout counter, or for a movie to begin, or, after putting his book down and turning off the bedside lamp, the giant pachyderm materializes, plants himself in front of Bob and there is no escape. Bob must then

confront the enormous beast's threat and find a way to live with it.

A few days later, just after he has switched off The News Hour and is heating up some lasagna for dinner, the phone rings–his movie-producer son Emmet is calling from Hollywood.

"Dad!"

"Emilio. que pasa?" Emilio Zaragosa' is a tongue-in cheek alias the Spanish-speaking Emmet has adopted.

"No mucho. Budgeting a couple of films–but God only knows if they'll ever be made, A director I've worked with has optioned one of the scripts but, honestly, he's such a ding-a-ling that I doubt he'll be able to raise the funds to produce it."

"Does sound as if you're putting bread on the table in the meantime. And how are Manda and Frida? You're the only family I have left." Bob almost immediately regrets having made the self–pitying remark but realizes that he is using every ploy possible to keep the elephant out of the conversation with his son.

"Frau Manda is fine, working on new design standards for the California Library System. And your granddaughter, Frida, she's on winter break and working as a part-time hostess at a local restaurant. She's got a new boyfriend and has just one more semester at Indiana, double majoring in music and psychology – but, Dad, what I called about is, what ever happened after they aborted that heart procedure?" The elephant is not to be kept at bay..

"Yeah, well, I have an appointment to see a specialist who is going to sort it out."

"Sounds mysterious, Dad, you're not holding out on me, are you?"

"No, I don't know anything definite yet–but I should after the appointment with the specialist."

"When's that?"

"November seventh."

"Dad!" Emmet's voice takes on a tone of urgency. "That's almost three weeks from now – can't he see you before then?"

"My thought, exactly. Originally, they tried to give me an appointment on November twenty-first. I had to use every sales tool in my kit to get them to squeeze me in earlier."

"Guess this specialist is in great demand, huh? So, what's his specialty?" The conversation is relentlessly driving Bob closer towards the elephant. How to escape?

'"Believe me, Emilio," he replies, disingenuously, his strained voice revealing the stress he is feeling. " I'm as impatient as you are to find out what's going on - but stewing about it is not going to help - I'm just going to have to wait a few more weeks for answers."

Actually, he's feeling ambivalent about the upcoming appointment. On the one hand Bob is still clutching to the slim hope that Hawks diagnosis will discover an innocuous cause of his condition, which can be easily treated, and cured. On the other, he fears that Rogerson's suspicion and the alarming consequences will be confirmed.

CHAPTER FOUR

After pulling into Brigham & Women's, Bob lumbers along the glassed-in overpass into the Shapiro Building. As he stops halfway to catch his breath and glimpse the vibrant street scene below, thoughts of the Bridge of Sighs in Venice crowd in. He feels as if he is a prisoner crossing over the bridge from the interrogation room in the Doge's Palace to the Prison, stopping to take one last view of beautiful Venice before being taken to his cell.

Once across he is directed to an elevator to the floor below and through a maze of double- door connected corridors into the Cardiology Imaging Center. The echocardiogram which follows has Bob lying bare chested on an examining table while a technician moves something like a computer mouse around his chest. All of which takes about twenty minutes after which he is escorted to a small room with a desktop computer and a couple of metal chairs. Dr. Hawk, he is told, is just finishing up his last surgery and will be along shortly.

Henry Hawk, MD, steps briskly into the small room. A tall, slightly portly man with a broad angular face. About 55 years old, Bob guesses. "Mr. Rosenbaum? "I'm Henry Hawk—you're a patient of Bill Rogers?" Hawk's voice still retains the pronounced British accent it had when he received his medical degree from Kings College, London, twenty-four years ago.

"Good to meet you... Dr. Rogers was about to perform a catheter ablation on me last month to correct my atrial fibrillation, when he discovered what he suspected could be amyloidosis. I believe he had my medical records sent to you. Hawk nodded,

looking down at an open file folder.

"Says here you are 79 years old—you certainly don't look it – and that you bicycle long distances and play tennis – that true?"

"Yes, except when I'm experiencing the a-fib, the irregular heartbeat. Then I can hardly walk across the room without feeling breathless."

"Well, let's see what's going on. I'll have a look at your echocardiogram. Have a seat here." Hawk sits down on a swivel chair in front of the computer, taps a few keys. A bright green image of Bob's heart with its chambers pulsing appears. Hawk closely examines the screen, successively clicking back and forth from different views and as he does, frowns and puts his index finger to his lips.

"What do you see?" Hawk swivels around, facing Bob and adjusting the monitor so they can both look at it.

"Here, you see those square white flecks. Typical of what we see in early stage AL.

"AL?"

"Amyloidosis. Of course, we'll have to confirm with more blood and urine tests, but there do seem to be AL deposits on the heart wall. Suddenly, Bob feels his whole world is spinning out of control. He is in completely new and terrifying territory. What is the meaning of what is going on? What is going to happen next?" He tries to pull himself together.

"So, what does that mean? How serious?" he asks, terror stricken. He is pretty sure he has already read the answer in Hawk's face.

"Well, first we'll have to confirm, with more lab work, that these flecks we are looking at are actually amyloids." Hawk is sensing Bob's reaction and feeling stress himself at having to

deliver this fateful news to Bob, and has assumed an increasingly unemotional tone.

"And what are amyloids?" Bob has a pretty good idea of what they are but wants to hear it from Hawk.

"They are little pieces of abnormal insoluble protein that deposit themselves on the heart walls and replace the normal heart muscle."

20

"And then what?"

"Well, Amyloidosis is progressive, and..." Hawk pauses, considers his patient's face and body language to decide how much further to take this. Bob's jaw appears clamped. He is perspiring slightly, and his hands are clenched. Hawk decides not to add – "in addition to irregular heartbeat, increasing shortness of breath, heart failure, even stroke can result." Instead, he says,

"Let's not let us get ahead of ourselves on this. I'll have lab results in a few days and then we can sit down and go over the situation. How does that sound?"

Bob is drained, like the accused, having listened to his lawyer's defense, relieved to have had his day in court come to an end. He remembers a reprimand he had received as a young officer in training, during war games after explaining that he had ordered a certain maneuver, assuming the enemy would do such and such.

"Never assume anything, Rosenbaum!" barked the seasoned commanding officer. It was advice Bob was eager to embrace at this juncture.

CHAPTER FIVE

The next Wednesday at 11:30 he is back in the examining room at Brigham & Women's awaiting Henry Hawk. Bob hasn't been sleeping well. Lying in bed he tries to convince himself that if he can just forget about his heart by concentrating on his breathing, fatigue will set in and allow him to drift off. Sometimes it works. When brief periods of sleep do come, they are filled with stressful dreams, seemingly unrelated to his medical condition. But, of course, the dreaming mind is a skillful conjurer, which can cleverly hide the real cause of anxiety in a disguised narrative.

In one dream, Bob finds himself at college, filled with helpless anxiety because he is unable to locate his course schedule, his classroom number and his textbook. The mind is not a one-trick pony, and amongst its tricks is a dream variation in which Bob leaves his coat and suitcase on a train only to be unable to retrieve them later at the train station's lost and found. Awakening, the details of Bob's dream wash away, leaving only helpless anxiety.

He reaches out to touch Hildy's body, always a comfort after a bad dream, only to realize she is no longer beside him, will never be there again, and he is filled with despair.

Before heading down the hall to consult with his patient, Henry Hawk feels nausea coming on, a sensation he invariably experiences before having to reveal a life-threatening diagnosis to a patient. Years ago, when he had had to do so for the first time, Hawk told

himself that, over time, he would get used to it and the discomfort would go away, but it never did. Today, as he approaches the consulting room he feels both depressed and apologetic, depressed because he is unable to provide Bob with a cure and apologetic about having to break the bad news to him. In his mind he rehearses the words he can use to tell Bob the truth while at the same time being sympathetic and supportive.

As Henry Hawk enters the consulting room, Bob studies his face, trying to read his expression for clues as to what the cardiologist is about to tell him but is unable to penetrate Hawk's non-revealing expression.

"How are you feeling?" Hawk looks up from an open file he is holding at Bob.

"O.K. I guess—actually a little ragged out," answers Bob. "I haven't been getting much sleep since our last meeting."

"Understood. Waiting to find out what is going on can be stressful. Mr. Rosenbaum—Bob, may I call you Bob?" Bob nods affirmatively thinking Hawk's request to address him on a first name basis suggests troublesome news is about to arrive.

"Bob, I've gone over the scans and lab tests and taken together they point to AL, Amyloidosis, protein deposits on the heart wall. I'm sorry to give you that news, but now that we know what we're dealing with, in an early stage, we will be able to treat the condition as effectively as possible". Bob grasps the arms of the chair he is sitting on for support. Up to this moment he has been able to defend himself against this imminent life threat, armed with the rationalizing that he may not actually have amyloidosis but now that this flimsy armor has been stripped away, he feels as naked and vulnerable as a man adrift at sea clutching but slowly losing his grip on a lifebuoy. His mind selectively seizes on the only encouraging words in Hawks last sentence, "treat the condition."

"Does that mean you can cure it– get rid of the amyloid deposits?" Bob asks, hopefully. Hawk replies in a muted voice.

"I wish I could tell you that we could. Our Amyloidosis Clinic and research associates have been working hard to find a cure and we are learning more about amyloidosis every day, but so far, we haven't been found a way to fully arrest the condition or to reverse

it." Bob's face falls, his hope of salvation dashed.

"That doesn't mean there won't be a breakthrough soon," the cardiologist adds reassuringly.

"So, what's the prognosis if there is no breakthrough?" Bob asks, anxiously.

"The amyloid protein builds up in tissues or organs, in your case on the heart wall."

"And?"

"Yes, well, as it builds up it begins to limit the heart's normal function - and ultimately, results in heart failure."

Bob slumps forward in his chair, cradling his head in both hands for half a minute. The realization that he has just been handed a death sentence shocks him and fills him with fear He can barely compose himself enough to croak,

"Ultimately. How long is ultimately?" The old Bob, the courageous Bob, would have been eager to know. The new Bob, unnerved and desperately seeking a reprieve, trembles with fear.

"Of course, that varies,"-answers Hawk. "The condition

progresses more rapidly in some patients —more slowly in others."

"O.K., O.K. but, on average, how long are we looking at?"

"If the condition remains untreated, the average survival time is about a year- but with treatment-bone marrow transplants and stem cell rescues, which are possible on patients in as good physical condition as you are, there's every reason to believe we can extend that time considerably."

"Considerably, meaning?"

"Well, some of our patients have survived for three to four years." Bob hears every word, but his mind resists processing the bad news. Hawk, sensing that getting his patient involved in his treatment immediately is going to be the best mental and medical approach says,

"Bob, we need to take some additional images to find if the amyloidosis is present in any other organs, so we can determine the most effective treatment. We can do the imaging today, here in the hospital, if you're feeling up to it, or if not, we can schedule it for

later in the week." Hawk looks up at Bob who emits a deep sigh. He's exhausted. There is no fight left in him.

"Hell, might as well get it over with today," he replies.

"Good." Hawk picks up the phone and arranges for the tests, scribbling authorizations on a couple of forms and hands them to Bob.

"Take these up to Radiology in Room 304. And when you're finished there stop by the blood lab in 208 and give them this slip. I'd like to see you next week when we'll have the results. We'll be able to get you started on treatment then. If you stop at the cardiology desk on your way out they will set up an appointment for you. And, Bob, cheer up. We're going to fight this thing together and we've got some pretty good weapons now in our arsenal and some new ones coming along. Hawk extends his hand and Bob grasps it as though it was a lifeline in a dystopian sea. He desperately wants to believe that the forthcoming treatments will buy enough time for new drugs or procedures which can save his life to become available.

CHAPTER SIX

Months later Bob, is at home, sitting at the Alvar Alto dining table, looking over Kingston Bay through the glass sliders of the midcentury modern house he and Hildy built. He downs a glass of orange juice, half fresh-squeezed, the other half from a Tropicana carton–Hildy's formula. Munching granola in skim milk, he spots a raft of mallards in their white, metallic green, and blue finery, sedately paddling by.

Breakfast is the least stressful part of Bob's day, the least changed by Hildy's absence because for years it has been his responsibility to feed Gonzalez the cat, brew the coffee and get the juice and cereal and milk or toast (with Chivers marmalade) on the table.

He continues to have *The New York Times* delivered. Both the routine of reading it daily and of having it confirm his own liberal views affords him comfort but, this morning, his encounter with the first page elicits an involuntary shiver. On the front page is a photo of George W. Bush flashing a V for victory and declaring the end of the military phase of the Iraq war.

Bob's day, which he purposefully plans to distract him from his loss and health concerns, are tolerable. Every Monday he makes an early morning trip to the Stop & Shop supermarket to stock up for the week. On Wednesday, an hour and a half hour Spanish conversation class at the Senior Center. On Tuesday, Thursday, and Saturday mornings, he drives to the gym in nearby Cordage Park to work out on a stationary bike and machines. Every other Thursday morning at eleven there is the Senior Men's Group's wine and cheese hour at one of the member's houses, and on Sunday mornings, in seasonable weather, a ride with the local bike group. In between he is researching for or writing "Think Green", a monthly column about sustainability, which he has written for years for The Schooner, the local newspaper. He fills in the afternoons with household chores and practicing songs from the American Song Book on his guitar and lately, because he has become sleepy after lunch, indulges in an afternoon snooze.

But at lunch and again at dinnertime there are no such diversions, and Hildy's absence becomes acutely painful to bear. Most days she would manage to get home at noon to rustle up lunch and they would discuss the highlights of their mornings and exchange their afternoon schedules. At 6 PM, with glasses of Sauvignon Blanc in hand they would plop down on the white leather living room sofa to watch The News Hour with Jim Lehrer on PBS. Then at 7 PM Hildy would put the finishing touches on dinner, serving it on the Alto table with the three-cylinder frosted-glass lighting fixture dimmed and the long beeswax candles in the pewter

candle sticks lit–Hildy always lit candles, no matter how simple the meal. Though alone now, and though he feels a little foolish doing so, Bob keeps up the ritual. The act of lighting the candles brings him the illusion that she is present, right there just beyond the arc of

light.

At first, right after Hildy's death, preparing dinner never seemed a strain. Hildy's lady friends would deliver soups, stews and casseroles regularly. But in time these deliveries fell off and as they did, he began eating out more frequently. But he felt uncomfortably self-conscious doing so. sitting alone at a table, reading his Kindle and feeling envious of couples and families

engaged in spirited conversation.

Once a week he went out to dinner with Jamie Kirk, an old friend. Kirk, a widower for twenty years, was happy to take a weekly escape from his own limited culinary repertoire to break bread with Bob and prattle over local news and gossip. Usually they met at the Horse & Carriage, a local hangout where Jamie, invariably, ordered a draft beer and the Carriage Burger, while Bob stuck with a glass of Pinot Grigio, green salad, and a mac and cheese. And there were usually weekly dinner invitations from friends, and while these meals satisfied his appetite and need to socialize, they neither filled the void of Hildy's absence nor allowed him to recapture the pride he felt about her beauty and sparkling personality, which shone at such gatherings or the even greater joy of quiet, intimate dinners alone, together.

The weekly dinner with Kirk and invitations from friends usually left Bob five evenings a week to fend for himself. It was not long before he began to rebel against the prepared food he had been buying at the supermarket. He vowed to start cooking his own.

First, he consulted the recipes in Hildy's cookbook collection, James Beard's *"American Cooking"*, Michael Fields' *"Culinary Classics"* and Julia Childs and Simone Beck's *"Mastering the Art of French Cooking"*. But he soon realized that all of them assumed a familiarity with basic cooking techniques about which he was clueless.

He mentioned his culinary plight one evening at friends, Liv and Peter Valente's, whereupon Liv left the dinner table, and, after rummaging through her kitchen shelf, returned with a well-worn volume titled" "How to Cook" with the encouraging subtitle "An Easy Imaginative Guide for the Beginner."

"This is just what you need" said Liv, putting the book on the table in front of him.

"When Peter and I were first married I had no idea of how to cook. So, Peter's mother gave me this book. Not a purely altruistic gift. She was probably concerned that her son might starve." Liv winked at Peter. "Anyhow, I think the book saved our marriage. You can keep it."

"Muchas gracias." Bob noted with relief that the author was male, one Raymond Sokolov whom Bob imagined might, at one time, like himself, have been uninitiated to the culinary arts.

There were six people at Liv and Peter's dinner table that evening, Liv's best friend, Carol, a divorcee, and a couple Bob had never met before who had recently moved into the community. As the evening progressed, Bob wondered if the couple had been invited as a cover for Carol who might have him in her sights. Carol was laughing more heartily than his marginally amusing remarks deserved, and, at one point, he thought he detected a come-hither look as she ran her fingers through her hair.

Not that there was anything wrong with Carol. After divorcing an alcoholic husband years ago, she had worked her way up to a position as a school administrator while, brought up Jason, who was now at Dartmouth, having gotten in on a scholarship. Carol had an all-American-girl face, a slim, curvy figure, and an ample bosom. He could easily imagine getting in bed with her but wondered what they would talk about over coffee the morning after. He suspected she might be a nudnik, a real bore.

A few days later, Bob and Carol bump into each another at the checkout line at Foodies, the local supermarket.

"Just picking up some fettuccine noodles, heavy cream, and Parmesan," says Carol. "I have a longing for Fettuccine Alfredo, decided to make it for dinner, tonight." Bob's eyes light up.

"Fettuccine Alfredo. My favorite pasta! I still remember the first

time I ate it."

"Really, well then, why don't you come over for dinner tonight – are you free?" Bob takes out his smart phone

"Have to consult my calendar." He pretends to be looking at the phone screen, then smiles sheepishly.

"Just kidding—sure I'd love to. Where do you live?"

"679 Franklin Street - know where Franklin Street is?"

"No, but Siri here does. What time?"

"Is seven O.K.?"

"You bet. Thanks. See you then." As they part Bob feels a sense of elation, having made his first date since Hildy's death, beginning to get on with his life, but then, quickly, he becomes apprehensive and nervous as a teenager about to go on his first date.

CHAPTER SEVEN

There are nice old farmhouses on Franklin Street but number 67 is not one of them. A typical '50s "Builder's Colonial," 67 Franklin is a mishmash of undersized trim, plastic shutters, and a low-sloped roof covered with scrawny asphalt shingles, not reminiscent of early

American architecture.

Bob presses the illuminated plastic buzzer and, momentarily, Carol opens the door. She is wearing a low-cut white peasant blouse and a knee-length floral-patterned skirt. As he hands her a gift bag of wine, he tries not to appear not to be staring at the ample swell of bosom above

her blouse, as he says, "The wine store recommended this dry chardonnay to pair with fettucine." When they get to the kitchen, Carol examines the bottle.

"I already have open bottles of red and white. I thought we could drink them now and

save your nice bottle for dinner. O.K.?"

"Sure, may I have a glass of the white?" Carol pours from the bottle into two tall-stemmed wine glasses, hands one to Bob, takes a sip from the other and puts it down on the kitchen counter. She checks the pasta, which has come to a boil, and begins tossing a green salad in a large wooden bowl.

"So, about your first fettucine experience?"

"How long until dinner?

"About fifteen minutes." Bob smiles.

"O.K. I'll give you the fourteen-minute version. Towards the end of the Depression, in the late '30's, my father and his brother ran a small advertising agency in Manhattan. But the economy had not recovered, their business had dried up, and they had to close shop. Our family was scraping by on my Dad's savings and a small inheritance of my mother's. They decided it would be cheaper to live touring around Europe for a year than to remain in New York City waiting out the recovery, so the three of us with our 1931 Ford Sedan, with a steel roof rack to hold our steamer trunks, sailed for Cherbourg. We stayed in Paris a while, in a small pension, visiting museums, castles, churches, and monuments. My mother, who had a degree from Teachers College, home schooled me with a young German college graduate who took on the duties of an au pair for the travel experience and opportunity to polish up her English.

In the afternoons, she took me to play in the Bois de Boulogne and the Luxembourg Gardens.

Eventually, we decamped Paris, working our way east across France to Austria and Switzerland, then south to Italy– Milan, Venice, Florence, and finally, Rome. For my birthday, my parents invited me to dinner at Alfredo's of Rome. By then, Alfredo di Lelio's restaurant, on the Via della Scrofa, had already developed a local reputation because of di Lelio's signature dish, fettucine Alfredo. The event, which raised the modest restaurant to international fame, came after the honeymoon visit of the silent film stars, Mary Pickford and Douglas Fairbanks. Before leaving Rome, the film idols presented de Lelio with the golden fork inscribed "To Alfredo–Douglas Fairbank" and a matching spoon, engraved "To Alfredo–Mary Pickford".

After nibbling on antipasti, we ordered the famous dish and when it was brought to table, and, according to tradition, the restaurant lights were dimmed while the fettucine was served with a flourish, using the now famous golden fork and spoon. So that was my introduction to fettucine Alfredo." Carol winks at him.

"Cool. So even as a young boy you were already becoming a man of the world." Carol lifts the cover of the pot with the pasta, adds a teaspoon of salt, butter, Parmesan cheese and a little water, and begins tossing the mixture. "Don't know if this will live up to your expectations. An old Martha Stewart recipe, one of Sam's favorite dishes," she says, immediately regretting that she has brought her ex into the conversation. "Anyhow, it's ready. If you'll open your bottle of white and bring in our wine glasses I'll bring dinner to the table."

By the time me he has uncorked the wine and brought the bottle and their glasses in, Carol has the pasta and salad on the table, has lit candles and switched off the chandelier.

"They say dinner always tastes better by candlelight," she says as she ladles out the fettucine and passes him the salad bowl. Bob twinges at the banality of her pronouncement and his eyes tear up as he is reminded of the quiet comfort of candlelit dinners he shared with Hildy, their intimate and meaningful exchange of ideas. Carol, noticing his discomfort asks, "Something wrong? Did I say something that upset you?"

"No, nothing." Regaining his composure, Bob pronounces the fettucine "outstanding!" and proposes a toast to Alfredo, but the dinner conversation soon becomes strained. After praising mutual friends and small talk, they are unable to find anything substantive to discuss. Carol chats about her Monday watercolor class and Wednesday bridge group. Bob enthuses about cycling with the bike group and working with Sustainable Duxbury to reduce fossil fuel waste.

Yet, though they are unable to find common interests, each is physically drawn to the other. Carol registers that Bob is taller and huskier than her ex, Sam, whom she always considered a little too thin and too short, the reason she avoided wearing high heels. She likes Bob's close-cropped beard and intrigued by the tuft of chest hair visible above his unbuttoned blue Oxford button-down shirt. For Bob, the candlelight has erased the fine age lines in Carol's face, making her look more youthful than she is. He feels a stirring of desire. Once the main course is over, Carol clears the table and reappears with two crème brûlées in hand.

"I have a confession to make. I didn't make these—picked them up at French Memories on the way home. Thought we could have coffee after, in the living room—do you drink coffee?"

"I do. Sounds perfect." When they are settled on the living room couch with demitasses of coffee, Bob says, "When I'm home, alone, after dinner I usually pick up a book, read for an hour or so or until I get drowsy. How about you?"

"I'm a movie freak, a sucker for romantic comedies. Darlene, my sister-in-law, she's hooked on them too. She has a Netflix subscription and after she's seen them, she passes them on to me to watch and mail back to Netflix. Haven't received one from her this week though, or we could have watched it tonight." Carol puts her fingers to her chin as her eyes assess Bob, and then dart across his face to rest briefly on his close-cropped hair and then inadvertently drop to the opening of his shirt at the chest and come to rest on his big hands. Her physical attraction to him makes her feel vulnerable.

"Maybe it's just as well that there's no movie, tonight." she says defensively. I have a yoga class at eight AM tomorrow. Need to get my beauty sleep." Bob senses that Carol is attracted to him and, possibly, untrustworthy of her emotions. He looks at his watch.

"It's almost ten—maybe we should call it a night, but I'd like to see you again. Do you by any chance like Japanese food?

"I love Sushi. What did you ask?"

"Thought I'd invite you to my favorite Japanese restaurant, Sushi Yoshi in Norwell. What do you say?"

"Yes, I'd love to. When did you have in mind?"

"How about next Tuesday, at seven?" She thinks for a moment.

"Tuesday is my least busy day. That would be fine." Carol walks him to the door. He plants a brotherly kiss on her cheek, hesitates, then impulsively draws her to him and their lips meet in a long, languorous kiss. Finally, she pushes back, flustered, pushes back he hair, trying to regain her composure.

"Slow down," she says.

"Sorry, guess I got carried away. Are we still on for Tuesday?"

She nods affirmatively. "O.K. I'll pick you up at seven. As he leaves Bob's heart is pumping rapidly with the excitement of the embrace and passionate kiss. But as he walks to his car the excitement of the passionate encounter subsides, morphing into a nagging sense of guilt at having just cheated on Hildy.

CHAPTER EIGHT

The following Tuesday evening at Sushi Yoshi they have settled in to a more comfortable relationship with each other sharing their mutual enthusiasm for Japanese cuisine and discussing their individual favorites. Towards the end of the meal, Carol mentions that she has received a new Netflix CD from her sister-in-law and asks Bob if he'd like to watch it. Bob, hoping a romantic interlude could also be in the offing readily agrees.

Just as they seat themselves on the couch in Carol's living room, she jumps up. "You know, I've got this bottle of Limoncello that I meant to serve us after the Fettucine dinner last week, but I completely forgot. I'll get us a couple of glasses now. Meanwhile, why don't you open the CD package and see what the film is? Bob opens the CD envelope.

"It's called 40 Days and 40 Nights, stars Josh Hartnett and Shanyn Sossman – never heard of either of them—did you?"

"No, can't say I have. But, we could give it a try, anyway."

Carol walks over to the TV, inserts the disc in the DVD player, turns down the lights, and before clicking the remote, kicks off her shoes and settles down on the couch next to Bob, tucking her legs under her. The movie turns out to be about a young dot.com employee whose obsession with a former girlfriend prevents him from having successful sex with any other women. His co-workers talk him into abstaining from all sexual activity for forty days and

nights to resolve his problem. Then they make side bets with one another as to how long he will be able to hold out.

As an explicit erotic scene between the hero and a new girlfriend starts to play out, Carol glances nervously at Bob and says, "Not what I expected. It's embarrassing."

"It is," he agrees while wondering if, in addition to being embarrassed, Carol is also becoming sexually aroused. He places his hand on her thigh, half anticipating that she will push it away. But, after a moment's hesitation, she rests her hand on his and gives it a slight squeeze and turns to him. They kiss, embrace briefly and he feels a strong surge of arousal. But then she pushes back, turns away from him running her fingers through her hair and says,

"Maybe we should get back to watching the movie." As she glances down to disengage their hands, she notices the bulge in his trousers.

"Oh my!" she giggles. Though momentarily disconcerted that his erection has been discovered he is overwhelmed with desire for

Carol passionately kissing her face, her neck then the fullness above her blouse.

"Can we turn off this stilly movie, Carol? I want you. She pushes him away gently, sits upright, considers briefly, and then clicks off the TV, takes his hand and leads him to the bedroom. He is elated but worried that he may not be able to perform. She thinks she can fake it if she doesn't respond but is concerned that he may be turned off by her no longer youthful body. They slip off their clothes their bodies meet in an embrace and then they settle down on the bed, exploring each other with curious fingers and needy lips. She draws his face up to hers and they exchange a long languorous kiss. She spreads her legs and guides him into her. They thrust into

one another slowly, tentatively at first, then quickening and with greater assurance. As Carol approaches climax, she uncontrollably bites Bob's ear. Unconsciously, he cries out "Oh-Oh! Oh Hildy" as he accelerates, ejaculates and is spent. Carol's body suddenly goes

limp. Bob looks perplexed.

"What happened?" he asks.

"What do you mean, what happened?"

"You went limp suddenly."

"Dam right I did. You're not surprised, are you?" He could sense her hostility.

"Let's talk about it." She props herself up on one shoulder.

"Talk about it? What's there to talk about. When you were close to orgasm you blurted out 'Hildy'. I realized immediately that you were making love to her not me, using me as a surrogate for your dead wife!" Carol turns away pulling the covers over her.

Bob is stunned, then feels a nauseating sense of guilt. He lies there unable to sleep, listening until he hears Carol's slow regular slumberous breathing. Then he gets up, quietly dresses and slips out of the house.

CHAPTER NINE

Bob's experience with Carol makes him face up the fact that he needs to wean himself away from his obsessive relationship with his dead wife and get on with his life. So, when his friend, Flash Peters calls proposing that they sail Bob's 14-foot catboat to a distant harbor on Cape Cod Bay, he enthusiastically agrees. The challenge, he feels may just be the antidote he needs to emerge from his fixation with Hildy and from his depressed state about his own mortality.

After the sailing venture ends, Bob finds that writing it up as a feature article for the local newspaper reinforces his feeling that he is making some progress in moving forward with his life. Here is what he wrote:

Two Men and a Cat

"Sometimes, the only way to get rid of an itch is to scratch it. That is what the two men in this chronicle did to relieve their itch. The author who at 78 is still cycling around Europe and shuffling around the local tennis courts and, Flash, my wiry companion, 70, who has climbed Kilimanjaro and completed over 1000 deep sea dives worldwide, were both ready for a new challenge. *El Gato* (The Cat), my 14-foot, gaff-rigged catboat, seemed indifferent.

The itch began to manifest itself soon after Flash casually asked me if it would be possible to sail *El Gato* from Kingston to Provincetown?" The itch became noticeably itchier as we speculated about making voyage in short hops from harbor to harbor along the inner crescent of Cape Cod, overnighting in Sandwich, Barnstable, and Wellfleet. But complications such as timing the tides, navigating unfamiliar harbors, and securing moorings and overnight accommodations convinced us to abandon that plan.

The plan we settled on, simpler but riskier, was to sail a straight-line course from the mooring off my house in Kingston directly to Provincetown. The distance was about twenty miles and we estimated that under ideal conditions that we could make the voyage in six hours. If we could get underway at dawn, we should be able to reach Provincetown and trailer *El Gato* and get back to Kingston before sunset. And, if skies were clear, we assured ourselves, we would be able to sight the Pilgrim Monument overlooking Provincetown Harbor after a few hours under sail and be able to use it to stay on course.

Admittedly, the contemplated passage would be less rigorous than that of Captain William Bligh of Mutiny of the Bounty fame. In 1789, Bligh, who was set adrift at sea and with a crew of eighteen men somehow survived a punishing seven week, 3,600-mile voyage to the island of Timor. If less demanding, our contemplated voyage from Kingston to Provincetown was still a considerable challenge. Bligh's boat, after all, had been twenty-three feet long as opposed to my fourteen-footer and both Bligh and his crew were experienced seamen. Bligh at thirty-five, was less than half my age, a happily married man with children and in good health.

To reach our distant destination before dusk, Flash and I determined we would need to get underway on an early morning's rising tide with fair weather and winds of five to ten knots from the North or South. Initially, it looked as though those critical elements, weather, tide, wind direction and wind speed would align on August 19th. But then, unaccountably, on August 17th, the forecast changed, and winds were predicted to drop to three mph in the morning, pick up in the afternoon and change direction to East, killers for the expedition.

A second window of opportunity opened up on September 3rd with a forecast of sun, scattered clouds, high tide at 8 AM, and a seven to ten knot breeze from the north and northwest for most of the day. Ideal conditions. This time the forecast held right up to the day of departure.

The plan was to drive my aging Honda Pilot, with *El Gato's* boat trailer attached, to Provincetown on September 2nd, the day before the sail.

After depositing the trailer and the Pilot in Provincetown, we had planned to take the 4:30 PM ferry from Provincetown to Plymouth where Flash's wife, Jodie, would pick us up. But a snag developed. Jodie's recorder group had a performance scheduled at Flash's house at 4 PM that day and both Flash and I were expected to attend. So, I drove the trailer out early in the morning with Flash tailing him in his Prius, and we drove home in time for the concert.

Things did not go as smoothly as anticipated in Provincetown. At the only public boat ramp in town an ordinance was posted, prohibiting leaving boat trailers in its parking lot. That hurdle was overcome when the head honcho at Flyers Boat Shop a couple of blocks away allowed us to leave the trailer (but not the Pilot) overnight in Flyers' tiny boatyard. Then a second complication developed. The parking lot at the ramp allowed parking for a maximum of only four hours. A phone call to the Parking Authority proved to no avail, so we left the Pilot in one of the parking slots, hoping that it would not be towed away by the time we arrived the following day.

At 5:30 on September 3rd, the following morning, My cell phone's alarm honked a wake-up call. I bounded out of bed, slipped into a pair of bathing trunks, T-shirt and old sneakers, made coffee, poured a glass of orange juice, filled a cereal bowl with Alpen and skim milk, put it all on a tray and sat down at the table on the deck.

The first hint of dawn, lighting a charcoal sky revealed glass-smooth water and the flag on a nearby dock slowly fluttering to the southeast, both encouraging signs.

At 6:30 the crunch of Flash's Prius tires on the driveway announced his arrival.

"El Jefe!" Flash bellowed, putting down his gear bag of equipment long enough to execute a smart salute.

"Comandanté !" I returned the salute, "The wind and the sea look auspicious for our mission. Need to use the facilities before we get underway?"

"Never miss an opportunity," the younger seaman replied as he darted into the powder room. When he emerged, I said, "O.K. lets go for it."

As Flash grabbed my equipment bag, I tucked the dinghy oars under my arm, and the two of us descended to the beach. I pulled the dingy in by its outhaul, while Flash carried the outboard down to the water's edge. After loading everything into the dingy, we rowed out to *El Gato* on its mooring.

The sunrise had placed a wavy, watery brushstroke of carmine across the horizon, producing magenta and chartreuse reflections on the mirror-like sea. Only the gentle dip of the oars and a woeful seagull's cry punctuated the dawn's silence.

Once aboard *El Gato*, with the dinghy securely tied to the mooring, the outboard clamped to its mount, and all gear stowed, we removed the sail cover, dropped the rudder and centerboard and hoisted the sail. Flash, swinging the rudder and adjusting the sheet, pointed the little sailboat east, into the rising sun and towards Saquish and the Gurnet, the last points of land we could expect to see before glimpsing the monument in Provincetown.

What Bob doesn't say in the article was that these last weigh points, unknowable seas, and hazards ahead and his limited skills to navigate them, seem like a metaphor of his own life's situation. In trying to relax his grip on Hildy's memory, he wonders, is he simply letting go of the only lifeline at hand and acting out a death wish? Willfully trying to escape these morbid thoughts, he continues the article.

It was 6:50 AM. The wind was now blowing a respectable four knots out of the northwest. Aside from a few curious sea birds, the two of us were alone on the bay as our craft inched steadily towards our first way point, three green navigational lights seaward of Gurnet Point. By 8 AM we were abreast of the Gurnet Lighthouse and, borrowing Flash's binoculars, I could clearly see the three lights lined up in the direction of Provincetown. He took over the

tiller and sheet as the lighthouse slipped past the port side to the stern. A few fishing boats passed us, pushing urgently out into the open waters, but I was unable to follow them, having to keep a sharp eye out for lobster trap floats. To avoid becoming entangled in their lines required constant maneuvering.

As winds picked up, the calm waters morphed into waves with swells rising from two to three feet and some to four feet high with white caps, causing the little cat boat to pitch and plow. Now I had to zig and zag to avoid spray coming in over the stern as the bigger waves crested.

About a quarter of an hour into these worsening conditions, Flash noticed water sloshing around the deck at our feet, more than could be accounted for by spray alone. Had we sprung a leak? Flash started bailing, but as fast as he dumped pails overboard, the water would reappear. Handing the sheet and tiller to Flash I crouched down on my haunches to investigate. One of the stoppers of the boats self-bailing system had popped out, allowing the following sea to push water into the boat. Sliding around the deck on all fours as the boat rolled back and forth, I was finally able to reinsert the stopper so the two could bail and sponge out the remaining water.

Not having eaten for several hours and having expended considerable physical and emotional energy, Flash and I became aware that we were both hungry and thirsty. But with the boat rolling in the waves, retrieving, unwrapping, and holding onto sandwiches proved undoable. So, we settled for a couple of power bars that Flash had brought along and washed them down with water from a thermos that was within reach. As the small sailboat continued to

climb and plunge, up and down in an unruly sea, I started to worry. No land in view. No boats in sight. Not even a lobster pot or a bird sighted in the last half hour. The realization of how isolated and completely on our own we were, began to sink in. I now felt inadequate and foolhardy at having committed to such a dangerous project. Both of us now sensed that to make it to our destination would depend on our limited sailing skills, perseverance and luck. Should the seas become still angrier, we wondered, would we be able to stay on course? What if we were dismasted? Unspoken, these thoughts were reflected in the grim expressions that now replaced earlier grins.

A foggy mist to the east had been preventing Flash's binoculars from penetrating the space ahead, but then, miraculously, at about 10 AM, the mist began to clear and the wave swells began to subside. Flash, who thought he was now able to pick out the Provincetown monument, handed me the binoculars and I thought I saw it too. By 11 AM the monument, though still no more than a faintly etched vertical line on the horizon, was undeniably visible.

As spotting our destination quieted my anxiety, I became aware of a pressing need to urinate. How to accomplish this with *El Gato* bobbing and dipping had not occurred to me in the planning phase of the voyage, and it became obvious that I could not stand up in the boat to pee over the side. I handed the tiller over to Flash and, still seated, grabbed a small bucket, peed into it, and carefully emptied the bucket over the leeward gunnel. Flash, either feeling the same need or simply used to availing himself of any opportunity, followed suit.

As we sailed on, the wind dropped, to about four knots, by Flash's estimate, still enough wind to nudge *El Gato* and its occupants slowly toward our destination.

As we were finally able to pick out the faint shoreline of the outer Cape, it became apparent that all the other boats were approaching and leaving Provincetown harbor from the south while we were approaching from the west. There appeared, however, to be no reason not to continue our west to east course straight into the harbor, so we stuck to our heading and broke out sandwiches. At about 1:30, the flaw in our course selection became apparent. Dead ahead, between us and the harbor, was a sand spit. It was couple of miles long, extending to the south, and five feet above sea level at low tide. We had missed it on the chart. Perhaps at high tide (6:27 PM that evening) we would have been able to slip over it as *El Gato* drew only two feet-eight inches of water with her centerboard down. But with high tide over five hours away that was not an option. So, we had to turn the sailboat to the south and sail parallel to the spit to reach its end, round it, and then head back north into the harbor. The error would cost us two more hours at sea.

Meanwhile, arbitrarily, the wind had shifted to the north and was now right on our bow as we turned and headed toward the harbor. The two of us consulted and, concluding that tacking back and forth up to the harbor would take several hours and put us at risk of arriving close to dark, decided to use the outboard motor. Our ancient Johnson, which had started so reliably in test runs days ago, chose that moment to become balky. At first it completely refused to catch,

even in response to Flash's vigorous pulls. Then, after he had adjusted the choke several times, it started up reluctantly, only to die again in ten to fifteen seconds. Finally, with much coaxing the old engine began to run continuously, though not without an occasional death-threatening cough from which it would recover at the very last moment.

The pier to the south of their boat ramp destination came into view and fifteen minutes later we arrived at the concrete boat ramp. At 2:50 PM, almost eight hours to the minute after our departure, Flash cut the engine, I raised the centerboard and we coasted onto the beach next to the ramp.

It is not quite the end of the saga. Flash tended *El Gato* at anchor while I climbed up the ramp to the parking lot and to my relief, found the Pilot in its parking slot, not ticketed. I drove it to Flyers' boatyard, hooked up the boat trailer, and drove back to the ramp.

However, I lacked the skill to back the trailer down the center of the ramp and after several failed attempts, let Flash try. When that didn't work, Flash suggested that we detach the trailer from the Pilot and walk it down the ramp. A lady swimmer, seeing our predicament, kindly volunteered to hang on to *El Gato's* bowline while Flash and I inched the trailer down the ramp. I backed the Pilot down the ramp and we reattached the trailer. With much pulling,

pushing, cranking and grunting we were finally able to secure El Gato onto its trailer and drive it up the ramp. The last steps, unclamping the mast's forestay, pulling out the pins in the tabernacle and folding the mast over onto the boom gallows and securing it, went more smoothly than expected.

Before pulling out, I got in the Pilot and asked Flash to check the brake lights on the trailer. I pumped the brake but no lights went on. Apparently, the line had gotten wet while the trailer was in the water at the bottom of the ramp and the system had shorted out. Unfazed, I whipped out a red bandana from my pocket and tied it to the end of the mast. There remained an hour and a half of daylight. If our luck held, and we were not pulled over by a state trooper for

not having trailer lights, we might still make it back to Kingston before dark. Just one more risk in a perilous enterprise. The two of us smiled at each other as Flash victoriously declared, "By God, we've done it!" Gratified but spent, we gave each other a resounding high five, eased ourselves into the Pilot, and headed home.

CHAPTER TEN

Summer's arrival and the sailing adventure have lifted Bob's spirits. Tennis, bicycling, Fourth of July celebrations, summer theater, walks in the woods, and swimming off his pebbly beach provide diversion. Physically, he is feeling well, though short of breath on Sunday group bike rides and he finds himself no longer able to maintain his usual position near the head of the pack.

At his quarterly check-up in September at Brigham & Women's, he brings up his increasing breathlessness with Dr. Hawk. The physician, after examining him and then comparing a new echocardiogram with an earlier one, tells him that his amyloidosis has progressed, which explains his increased shortness of breath. Hawk proposes to treat the condition symptomatically with a diuretic to remove excess fluid from around his heart and lungs and a blood thinner to facilitate blood circulation. Though grateful that Hawk is taking positive steps to deal with his condition, these new reminders of the slow but unrelenting advance of the insidious disease eat away at his spirits.

In defense, Bob throws himself into gym workouts, writing his newspaper column, household chores and social gatherings, but none of those activities hold back the rising tide of depression that is engulfing him. And in his depressed state, he is drawn back into contemplating the darkest episodes in his life and how he may have unconscionably contributed to their tragic outcomes. How could Susy, the beautiful, vivacious, young woman he had first married, have slipped from social drinking into alcoholism and then so mentally disordered that she drove to a friend's house convinced that someone evil was pursuing her. What could explain what had befallen their third son, Andrew? A high-spirited high school soccer star, whose mental problems began to emerge after getting into Oberlin on an athletic scholarship. Warning signs showed up soon after his arrival on campus, such as his refusing to play on the soccer team and his becoming overweight. After graduation, Andrew landed a job with a New York brokerage firm but was fired shortly because of temper tantrums. Despite years of psychological counselling thereafter, shortly after Susy's death, he had become delusional and eventually ended his life by stepping off the station platform in front of an onrushing train. When the shock of his sudden death had subsided enough for Bob to think about it rationally, he realized that Andrew's suicide had not been a spontaneous move but one carefully planned, calculating the exact time, direction and speed of the express train would be hurtling past the station platform. The realization of for how deep the anguish Andrew must have suffered and for how long to have conceived and executed such a plan, only added to Bob's feelings of guilt and remorse at not having been able to prevent the tragedy.

Finally, there was the loss of his fourth and youngest, Carl. When Carl, as an undergrad at Columbia, had come out, Susy refused to believe he was gay, was never able to accept her son's homosexuality. Bob, though not completely understanding, was able to be supportive to Carl. But it was no less painful to think about him. After graduation the talented and ambitious Carl had gotten job in the men's clothing department of Bergdorf Goodman and was working his way up to become the men's clothing buyer for Bullock's Wilshire and then for Nieman Marcus. He had entered into a stable relationship with a partner and bought a nice house in Dallas. But Carl's promiscuousness along the way had resulted in an AIDS infection and before he could fully enjoy the life he had created, he had become ill and suffered a long debilitating decline. During most of it he maintained a courageously cheerful spirit, shielding those close to him from his suffering. In the last throws of the disease in the hospital, with Bob and Hildy at his bedside, he opened his eyes briefly, was able to look at them lovingly and say, quietly, "It is time to say goodbye."

All through these tumultuous times, Hildy had been with him, his reliable anchor to windward, keeping him stable and secure, and able to ride out the storm—and now when he needed her most?

At times like this, when reflecting on these misfortunes and on his present condition, Bob is so overwhelmed by negative feelings that he actually contemplates suicide and begins exploring ways he can end his life. Briefly, he considers a pistol to the head but rejects the idea for fear that if he might botch the job only to survive in a vegetative state. Drowning is another option he considers, and rejects as well. As a strong swimmer, he doubts he will be able to pull it off. A lethal injection or anesthesia he reasons would be easier and surer, but how could he ever get one? He also dismisses the idea of an OD of sleeping pills remembering that his sister, Amelie, with advanced cancer, had tried ending her life that way, only succeeding in putting herself in a coma from which she emerged to endure more suffering. The most painless practical method he finds is carbon is monoxide poisoning. Compared to the alternatives, it strikes him as the least painful, and easiest to pull off.

Carbon monoxide, he reads, replaces oxygen in the red blood cells and soon causes death. Simple. Bob figures he can accomplish that simply by running a length of flexible vacuum cleaner hose from his car's exhaust pipe into his car, closing the car windows and doors and turning on the ignition.

Having settled on a feasible way of exiting life puts Bob in a state of depressed calm. It is in this subdued mood that he shows up at a small dinner party being given by his friends, Sally and her husband John. Sally, noticing that Bob's usual funny observations and joi de vivre seem to have abandoned him, calls him aside saying "Bob, you don't seem yourself tonight. Are you feeling O.K.?"

"Well, actually I had a physical checkup on Monday and the doc says my engine is still good for a lot more miles, if that's what you're getting at." He says, thinking there are not a hell of a lot of miles left, and then Sally is pretty sure she has got her teeth into something and is not about to let go.

"Bob, I can see you're feeling miserable and if you are physically O.K., well then, maybe you should see a psychotherapist. When John and I have needed that kind of help, we've seen a fellow named, Gregory Ransahoff. We think he's pretty good." Bob is taken aback, aware now that he has not been able to conceal his inner turmoil.

"Didn't know my feelings were showing that much. Let me think about it, Sally. Maybe it's not a bad idea. Thanks for the suggestion - and for a nice evening. I hope I didn't spoil it for everyone."

"Don't be silly, Bob, of course you didn't. Hope you're feeling better. And, take care, Bob." Feeling grateful for his friends' concern he adds "Thanks again, Sally. Thanks, Fred. See you guys soon."

CHAPTER ELEVEN

The following morning, just as he finishes tidying up after breakfast, Bob's phone rings. John, his last night's host, is on the line.

"Hi, Bob – good seeing you last night – how are you doing?"

"O.K., John, what's up?" An awkward silence follows before John replies. "So, I thought I'd give you the phone number of the guy Sally mentioned last night, the psychotherapist – you know, just in case you wanted to get in touch with him." From John's hesitancy, Bob intuits that Sally probably put him up to making the call.

"Yeah well, thanks, John – very thoughtful of you."

"Got something to write on?" Bob reaches for the Post-it note pad and a stick pen.

"Yup"

"His name is Gregory Ransahoff and his phone number is 508-442-9876. His office is in Cordage Park, in Plymouth."

Thanks, John, much obliged," Bob answers, trying to mask his lack of enthusiasm.

"Stay in touch."

"Will do." Bob hangs up. He resists the idea of seeing a psychologist feeling that his inability to dig himself out of his depression this long after Hildy's death is a sign of weak character. But after the wave of instinctive rejection passes over, he realizes that, stuck in a morass of despondency, he is unable to extract himself on his own. And John, in nudging him to seek counseling had not known about the other more recent cause of his depression, the amyloidosis problem, something Bob was not about to reveal to John or Sally.

If only Hildy was still with him, dispensing her calm empathy he would be able to deal with his medical situation. But Hildy is gone and the more he thinks about the bête noirs that are stoke his thoughts of suicide, the more he convinces himself that he does need professional help.

On arriving at Ransahoff's, office Bob's feeling that seeking psychiatric help in his situation is a sign of personal weakness, returns, overlaid with skepticism about the effectiveness of psychiatry itself.

Ransahoff's modest suite in Cordage Park, is in an old brick rope factory built in the Italianate style in the late 1800s which has been remodeled into office spaces. Ransahoff's suite consists of two rooms, his office and a small reception room. When Bob arrives for his appointment he finds the receptionist's desk occupied by a buxom blonde in a dress which fits her like shrink-wrap.

"Can I help you, she squeaks in a stereotypical 'dumb blonde' voice.

"Name's Bob Rosenbaum – I have an appointment with Dr. Ransahoff at eleven."

"He'll see you in a few minutes – have a seat, please" After a few minutes, the door to the doctor's office opens and a tallish woman in a wide brimmed panama, wearing big sunglasses, strides past him on her way out of the reception room. He picks up the scent of a subtle perfume, Chanel No. 5. Bob is unable to get a good look at her, but something about her elegant figure and long stride seem vaguely familiar to him. A movie star? Someone he knew a long time ago? Who is she, this attractive mysterious woman?

His speculations are interrupted by the receptionist. "The doctor will see you now."

Ransahoff's small office which has a large window covered by drawn, rose damask drapes is furnished with a chaise longue and a side chair in the same fabric.

Ransahoff is short, rotund, bald, and his cheeks are so rosy as to suggest hypertension. He is perched on a Herman Miller Aeron desk chair that looks as incongruous as he does behind an elaborately carved reproduction mahogany desk. Except for the chair, the room suggests a parlor in a high-class bordello. On the desktop is a long triangle of rosewood with a brass nameplate on which is engraved, "Carpe Diem". Bob is about to ask what the Latin words mean when Ransahoff clears his throat.

"Zo vut brinks you here dis morning, Mr. Rosenbaum?"

"I'm depressed. I seem to have lost my energy and life doesn't seem worthwhile."

"Haf you consulted anyone about dis before, Bob, may I call you Bob?"

"Bob is fine, and no, I haven't seen anyone about this before, because in the past I've seldom been depressed – but six months ago my wife was killed in an automobile accident and more recently I've been diagnosed with an incurable disease."

"Zo doz are goot reasons vor you to be depressed, Bob, unt maybe I can help you – vee vill see. Tell me more about your relationship mit your vife unt how long it hass been zince you lost her,"

"Hildy and I were married in 1987, nineteen years ago – a second marriage. We were happy together, not that we didn't have our moments at swords points, but, all-in-all, it was a good marriage. We supported each other." Bob reflects momentarily on how, when in a crisis, Hildy would wrap him in the warm blanket of her calmness, steadying his volatility enough to get him through. Ransahoff continues.

"Unt how long ago vos de accident?"

"It's going on a year now. Seems as though it was yesterday, " he replys in a melancholy tone.

"Ya, vell iss not abnormal for you to still be griefing – unt vut about dis disease?"

"Well, I have been diagnosed with a condition called amyloidosis. It's a gradual build-up of protein deposits on the heart wall which is irreversible and ultimately brings on heart failure and death." Bob feels a sudden sense of relief of having unburdened himself of his worst fears and at the same time defenseless at having revealed them to this complete stranger.

"Ya, but, Bob, dis could be von of dose diseases, like prostate cancer in men over seventy vich develop zo slow dat you die from natural causes long before the disease gets you. All of us, vee are going to die, Bob, unt none of us knows ven."

Bob frowns, putting his hand on his forehead.

"Well, in my case I have a pretty good idea, when – the average life expectancy for those who have this disease is three to four years."

"I zee." Ransahoff shifts the subject." So tell me, vut iss your occupation, Bob?"

"I am retired. I was Marketing Manager for Douglas Hunter. They make all kinds of window shades and blinds. They had a mandatory retirement policy, sixty-five and you're out. I was sixty-five in 1992."

"Unt so vut do you do now mit your time?"

"When I retired, I took up writing. Freelanced for periodicals, magazines for a while. Now I write a bylined monthly column for the local newspaper."

"About vot?"

"About health and fitness, physical and mental health."

"Zo maybe you should be zitting at my desk unt I should be on de couch."

Bob is not amused at Ransahoff's attempt to lighten up the conversation. He looks nervously at his watch. They are more than halfway through the allotted time for the session.

"Your parentz, are dey alive?"

"No, they have passed on."

"Unt vat was your relationship mit your mutter?"

"I was her son."

"Please to repress your humorous instincts, Mr. Rosenbaum. Did you haf a close, loving relationship mit her?"

"Sorry, Doc, but I don't see what that has got with my being depressed because of losing my wife and having been diagnosed with a fatal disease."

"Vell vee vill get to zat in due time. So how was it between you and your mutter?" Ransahoff seems to be on auto pilot. Over the next half hour Bob is questioned about his parents, his first marriage and his children. And then the discrete chime sounds signaling that the session is over.

"I would like to zee you next week. Please to make an appointment on your vay out."

On the drive home, Bob, mentally replays the session he has just come from with Ransahoff, realizes that he still feels responsible for not having been able to prevent his first wife Susie's disintegration and sons Andrew and Carl's death. He also realizes that when he had revealed these feelings to Hildy, despite her own insecurities, had been able to keep Bob's at bay, running emotional interference for him, enabling him to continue to move forward with his life. But now, there was no one to block or run interference, he was on the field, unguarded, with guilty feelings closing in on him, and finding himself an inadequate open field

runner.

CHAPTER TWELVE

In Ransahoff's reception room a week later at the same time the mysterious woman he still cannot place, rushes out just before Bob enters the bordello-like office and seats himself in front of the psychiatrist's desk.

"Zo", begins Ransahoff, "How have you been doing zince I zaw you last veek, Bob? Are you feeling any better?"

"To be honest, I'm not getting much sleep. I don't feel like getting out of bed in the morning, and once I am up I don't feel like doing much of anything."

"Ya vell dat's because you are depressed." Bob's face flushes with anger. He didn't come here at $200 a session just to be told what he already knows.

"Doc, I understand that I'm depressed. What I came to see you about is how do I get out of my depression."

"Ya, ya, of course. Please calm yourself, Bob. Did you notice de sign on my desk?"

"Yeah, I was meaning to ask you about it last session and then the bell rang. In the meantime, I looked up Carpe Diem on Google - seems it's Latin for "Seize the Day.""

"Bob, it iss from one of Horace's Odes unt de full sentence iss 'Carpe Diem, quam minimum postero' but dat vuss too long to put on a little desk sign. The meaning iss 'Seize de day vile trusting little on vot tomorrow might bring'. In your case, Bob, I dink dot might be a goot vay for you to start living your life from now on." Bob reflects on what the psychiatrist has just said and reconsiders. Maybe this guy is not a phony.

"O.K. doc, I think I get it, but I can't seem to find the will or energy to 'seize the day'. I wasn't able to yesterday. I'm not able to, today and I don't see how I am going to be able to, tomorrow."

"Ya, ya, I understand. Zo let me put it to you like dis. It iss like you are at de bottom of a deep hole in de ground. Unless someone brinks you a ladder, you haf no way to climb out from de hole. O.K., zo maybe I can bring you a ladder, but de ladder iss not going to get you out from the hole unless you climb up the ladder yourself. Understand?"

"I think I understand what you're saying – you can give me the equipment I need to climb out of my depression but I'm going to have to climb out on my own"

"Prezisely."

"So, seeing as I have no will or energy to climb, how is the ladder going to help?"

"Goot question, Bob. Zince you ver not always depressed, you are going to haf to rediscover your enthusiasm for life unt dat vill gif you de energy to climb de ladder."

Bob shoots the psychiatrist a disbelieving look.

"And how the hell am I going to 'rediscover my enthusiasm' to get my energy back? Sounds like a Catch 22."

"Ya dot iss vot vee are going to work on together in deez sessions"

The chime rings signaling that this appointment is at an end.

CHAPTER THIRTEEN

After several more sessions with Ransahoff, Bob concludes he has extracted as much insight into his depression as he is going to get from the psychotherapist. His takeaway is that he needs to reclaim as much as possible of his former wellbeing, drawing any nurture and

support he can get from family and close friends. "Stuff that I ought to have been able to figure out on my own, without shelling out $200 a session to Ransahoff," he tells himself. Whatever the reason, Bob senses he has regained a little of his self- reliance.

Before the sessions, he had been on the point of cancelling the reservation in Mexico he had made for his annual winter escape with Hildy, but now he reconsiders. As awkward and painful as going back alone may prove, Bob reasons that he ought to as a first step to getting used to his new life circumstances.

In the meantime, the new echocardiogram and blood tests that Dr. Hawk has had him take have yielded disappointing results. More protein deposits are showing up on his heart wall, meaning that the disease is progressing. Hawk says he wants to see Bob when he gets back from Mexico to talk about a new stem cell rescue procedure, or alternatively, of taking part in a clinical trial of an experimental drug treatment. To Bob, it sounds as if Hawk is grasping at straws.

A few days later Bob's phone rings. It's Dodi Demaris, Hildy's Yoga teacher who recently lost her husband. She is calling to suggest that Yoga might help Bob readjust to his new life circumstances offering him a free trial Yoga lesson. Bob, who feels as though he is doing no better than just treading water accepts, figuring he might as well give Yoga a try. The free trial turns out to be a private lesson in a small carpeted room in Dodi's Plymouth studio. Dodi is wearing a skin-tight top and tights revealing a diminutive, wiry body. At first, she has Bob do a few stretches and standard yoga poses, but as the session progresses, a number of the poses seemed to require Dodi to press her body against his to help him maintain the position. It becomes unclear to him as to whether this is legitimate Yoga instruction or an invitation to something more. Towards the end Dodi has him lie still and close his eyes as she lights a stick of incense, waving it over him repeatedly while mumbling incantations in an indecipherable language which he later decides is probably Sanskrit. At the end of the session she invites him to a follow-up session. He thanks her graciously for the invitation but never goes back.

Bob is on his way to Mexico. The first leg of the trip lands him in Mexico City. Just walking up the jetway's incline into Terminal

2, he experiences such shortness of breath that he is forced to stop hallway up the ramp and move aside to let other passengers by. On previous trips, breathing had always been a little more labored in Mexico City, where, at a 7200-foot elevation, the air is much thinner than at home. But this time he feels different. He wonders, *has the amyloidosis really advanced enough to compromise his ability to breathe to this degree, or is he just experiencing a combination of elevation, jet lag, air pollution and, a touch of paranoia?*

By the time he gets to the baggage carousel, all the other passengers with checked baggage are already there, milling around, impatiently waiting for their luggage to appear. Finally, a jarringly loud doorbell sound signals the bags are about to arrive.

On the long trudge to the taxi stand, Bob spots an ATM machine and decides to get some pesos from it with his debit card. But, the machine balks, displaying a notice that his card is invalid. It's happened to him before in Mexico when the ATM has simply run out of money, but which its bank is unwilling to acknowledge. So typically Mexican he muses as he finds another ATM which readily accepts his debit card. Bob soldiers on, pausing every fifty steps or so to catch his breath. He stops briefly alongside the Wings Café which brings back memories of Margaritas and nachos with Hildy between flight connections. He swallows, takes a deep breath and moves on past narrow boutiques with women's fashions, jewelry, watches, artisan crafts, and souvenirs to the taxi booth where he buys a cab ticket for the hotel in which he plans to overnight before flying on to Puerto Escondido.

"Quiero ir al Hotel Catédral" he tells the driver in his best Spanish.

"Si senor, Hotel Zocalo Central" replies the driver.

"No, no – Hotel Catédral – es en Callle Donceles, detras La Catédral.

"Ah, Hotel Catédral, si, si senor, claro."

Bob wonders whether the cabbie actually misunderstands him or isn't paying attention or is simply playing a little gringo game with him.

They take off on a ramp that deposits them on a multi-lane highway through a grungy and seemingly endless urban sprawl. Then, after many twists and turns, they find themselves enmeshed in creeping rush-hour traffic. Finally circling the expansive plaza surrounding the massive grey stone Cathedral, they reach the hotel.

The Hotel Catedral is an aging dowager who has tried to recapture her youthful charm with a facelift, modish adornments, and a new hairdo. If the result is not completely successful, one still has to admire the old girl's plucky efforts to reprise her youth.

Only a few of the tables of the Hotel Catédral's restaurant are occupied. The place reminds him of an old Friendly's in the States – one in need of some TLC. Looking over the menu at the entrance, briefly, Bob considers going in and ordering a Margarita and the enchiladas suizas, but then, remembering that on his last visit, the Margaritas were too sweet and the enchiladas too rubbery, decides this is not the way to enjoy his first evening in Mexico. So, he hops a taxi in front of the hotel and tells the driver to take him to Fonda El Refugio, the restaurant he and Hildy discovered years ago in the Zona Rosa.

El Refugio occupies the first and second floors of a small loft building. What makes the building stand out from the others is that it is wedged between is the restaurant's Spanish colonial facade and the portion of the building above the facade which is painted a saturated purple-blue. Somehow, El Refugio, at night, with its white stucco exterior, wrought-iron gated windows, and eyebrow of terracotta roof tiles, manages to give the illusion of an old bar in a dusty, rural Mexican town. In the warmly lit interior, patrons, mostly locals and a smattering of tourists, are settled into burnished ladder-backed chairs at tables with peach-colored linens. On white stucco walls hang highly burnished old copper pots and pans and hung from the ceiling are large metallic red, green, and silver glass balls - Christmas ornaments on steroids. Taken altogether they impart a homey and festive atmosphere that Bob savors before being led to a small table alongside one of the walls.

A short, rotund waiter limps up to the table and there is a joyful moment of recognition. Bob rises and extends his hand to the waiter, who, visibly pleased, grasps it and shakes it vigorously.

"Que gusto verte de nuovo, senor".

Bob, whose Spanish is a little shaky, manages, "Yo siento lo mismo" hoping that it expresses that he is equally happy to see the waiter. Neither knows the other by name nor can they communicate beyond a few words in each other's language, but there is an unspoken bond between them. It is palpable—a non-verbal sharing of sensibilities and values – that strange emotional tie between two near strangers which defies explanation. Asking about Hildy he

"Su esposa no esta contigo, senor?"

Bob swallows hard before replying, "Ella esta muerte"

"Muerte? Que desastre!" The old waiter's face drops. Lamento mucho tu perdida." Bob does not need to understand the words. The expression on waiter's face says it all. If the purpose of this trip is to cast off his obsession with Hildy and make a new start, this first encounter is not an auspicious beginning.

"Gracias." Bob pulls himself together, orders a frozen Margarita. While waiting for it to arrive, he looks around the dining room. At the round table nearby, three Mexican businessmen are obsequiously attentive to the fourth, who is holding forth, obviously the boss. At a table for two along the wall a handsome young couple are holding hands across the table, staring soulfully into each other's eyes. It reminds him of the time he and Hildy sat across from one another at a similar table in a small Italian restaurant in Larchmont, the flame of their passion for one another like a ring of fire, isolating them from the world beyond. In time, the fire would become less

intense but continue to burn. Cold gusts of circumstance and conflict would sometimes threaten to extinguish the flame, but never did.

Bob's Margarita arrives, He sips it. It's chilled and a perfect blend of sweet and sour, with the triple sec and lime juice allowing just a hint of the tequila to emerge.

Bob savors the drink and contemplates. What tastes, sweet and sour lie ahead tomorrow in Puerto Escondido?

CHAPTER FOURTEEN

Bob steps off the plane in Puerto Escondido after an hour and a half flight from Mexico City. He hopes he can breathe more easily now that he is at sea level. But whatever advantage he may have gained from the lower elevation is sucked away by the sun's scorching heat radiating off the tarmac and the oppressive humidity. Shouldering his backpack in the blaze, he struggles across the tarmac, stopping twice to catch his breath before reaching the benevolent shade of a row of palm trees alongside Puerto's small modern terminal.

A white airport colectivo van brings him to the shaded Spanish colonial arched stucco entrance of the Santa Fe Hotel. The hotel's gaunt, leather faced, old gardener, Manuel, appears and carries his suitcase to the Talavera tiled reception counter. Maria Hernandez, the Santa Fe's manager, recognizes him, rises and, beaming, plants a kiss on both of his cheeks.

"Buenvenidos, Senor Rosenbaum." Hildy and he have stayed at the Santa Fe for so many years that arrival feels like an annual homecoming.

THE END GAME

Bob is relieved to be able to cross the hotel's grounds to his room without immediately running into friends or acquaintances to whom he would have to explain Hildy's death. At this hour, they are on the beach or taking their afternoon siestas. Bob unpacks, draws the drapes across the tall window and, after turning on the ceiling fan, drops down onto the king-size bed and closes his eyes. He feels alone and insignificant, but before he can dwell on those feelings, exhaustion overcomes him and he falls asleep.

Just before sunset on every evening, as if by magic, the Hotel's guests materialize on the hotel terrace to watch the sun's apricot orb sink slowly into the Pacific. Singles, couples, and groups stake out plastic chairs positioned to get the best view and are ordering their sundowners. It's a ritual and an opportunity to socialize for those who haven't been doing so for most of the day.

Bob spots the regulars, Chicago businessman Lenny and his wife, Dottie, the watercolorist with Richard the architect/kite flyer and his wife, Rosalind, the photographer at the far end of the terrace. They are heavily engaged in conversation. While he is trying to figure out how to go over to them to say hello without losing his chair, he hears a familiar female guttural voice behind him, unmistakably British, unmistakably aristocratic. It could only be that of Jane Dwight-Sanders, or, to be more precise, Lady Dwight-Sanders, wife of Rick Dwight-Sanders, member of the House of Lords.

"Well, now, here you are, Robert!" bellows Dwight-Sanders. "I had it in mind that you and Hildy were due here yesterday but when you failed to arrive I began to worry that something terrible might have befallen you, so I checked with Carmelita at the front desk–but she thought you were arriving tomorrow. Charming girl, Carmelita, but not the brightest crayon in the box, that one. Anyhow, here you are, Robert, so all is well. Ricky is due in first of the week, so we will have a jolly get-together. Where is Hildy? Under the weather after

the trip, poor dear?"

Jane pauses to sip from a tumbler she has brought from her room. Scotch, Johnny Walker Black Label, the only brand she and Rick drink. Bob remembers having spent the better part of the day searching the city of Oaxaca's wine and liquor shops trying to find that brand before a brief visit of the Dwight-Sanders to the City the year before.

Bob explains to Jane about Hildy's death, reluctantly, but also with a sense of relief, confident that within hours, Jane will have disseminated the sad news to all interested parties in the hotel, on the beach, and beyond, to the farthest reaches of Puerto, relieving him of that painfully burdensome chore of having to discuss it with them individually. But he's not able to get off Scott free.

Jane, who is becoming a bit leather- tonged after revisiting the Johnny Walker several times, says,

"I've arranged to have dinner here this evening with Austin and Gizelde Ramsey. Not sure you know them. They usually come in February and by that time you and Hildy are in Oaxaca." Realizing she has misspoken, she covers her eyes with her hand and says, "Sorry, you poor man, losing your beloved Hildy." Her face brightens. "You must join us for dinner—a charming couple, the Ramsey's – neighbors of ours in Marylebone- I know you'll enjoy them."

But he and the Ramseys have little in common to discuss so as soon as Bob has forked down the last morsel of his apple strudel, he excuses himself, pleading travel fatigue, and retires to his room.

CHAPTER FIFTEEN

Jane Dwight–Sanders puts her cup of tea down on its saucer and turns to Bob. "What I forgot to tell you last night, Bob—you know I think I am losing my mind – can't remember a thing." Bob smiles indulgently.

"Nonsense, Jane, you are not losing your mind. What is it you were going to tell me?"

"Oh yes – well, you see, I met someone you know, possibly an old flame of yours" Jane batts her eyes. "She was here at the Santa Fe last week with her sister and brother-in-law.

"What's her name?"

"Colette Connelly. She gave me reason to believe that you two may have once been 'an item'. That so?" Jane looks over her reading glasses to appraise Bob's reaction.

"A real stunner, Colette," adds Jane. I must say, you've got good taste, when it comes to the ladies.

"Coco?" gasps Bob in disbelief as he experiences a moment of elation followed by the same deep pang of loss he had had felt when, as a twenty-year-old Marine Lieutenant, his marriage proposal had been rejected by Coco.

"Coco" he repeats. "I can't believe it. She's alive and she was here at the Santa Fe? Jane, how on earth did you discover that we knew each other?" Not wanting to reveal to Jane how deeply moved he is by the news, he attempts to dissemble by adding, teasingly, "And you, Detective Dwight-Sanders, conjecturing that you were losing your mind."

"Well, you see, Bob we were having a casual conversation besides the pool, you know, small talk, girl talk, and I happened to mention that her brother-in-law's looks reminded me a little of an American friend of ours – you, of course! Well, Colette appeared dumbstruck and said something like, 'I did know a man named Bob Rosenbaum, but that was a lifetime ago. Probably not the same man. After all, there are millions of Bobs out there and Rosenbaum is a common name. This Bob Rosenbaum, how old is he?' "I'm not a good judge of age" I told her, "but he must be in his seventies." Jane peers at Bob again over her glasses for verification. "Did he mention where he went to school, or college, or if he was in the service?"

"I'm not sure if Bob said where he had gone to school, but he did say that, as an undergrad, he went to Yale. And I explained to her that you had told us colorful tales about your experiences in the Marines. Apparently, that was more than enough to convince her

that you were the Bob Rosenbaum out of her past and she added that you had dated in high school and, inadvertently, blurted out that she thought at the time that she was in love with you. Then as if to counter what she had just said, added something like, "At that age, love is so much about fantasies and hormones." Colette told me that after high school you had gone to Yale and she to Cornell and then that you had joined the Marine Corps and that the two of you had drifted apart. Bob, I'm not sure why she told me all this. After all, we had just met – but, once she got started there was no stopping her."

At that moment Bob and Jane's conversation is interrupted by Dottie, the Chicago watercolorist. When Dottie leaves, Bob asks Jane if she has any idea where Coco intended to go from the Santa Fe?"

"I'm pretty certain I do," replies Jane. "You see, her brother-in law told me the three planned to spend a couple of weeks in Oaxaca– asked me if I knew of a good hotel in the Historic District of the city, near the Zocalo. Actually, I couldn't remember the name of the nice little hotel Ricky and I stayed at in Oaxaca – it must have been at least four years ago– so I phoned Ricky that night and he remembered the name. There–I've forgotten it again, but I have it written down here in my little notebook. I'd be lost, completely lost, without my notebook." Jane puts on her reading glasses.

"Yes, here it is, The Hostal La Noria."

Bob knows the place well—an attractive small hotel, a couple of blocks east of the Zocalo. "Nice place, good location and reasonable," he responds. Bob feels there is nothing to be gained by reminding Jane that it was he and Hildy who had recommended the Noria to the Dwight Sanders in the first place.

The possibility of finding Coco in Oaxaca excites Bob and makes him inpatient for his short remaining time in Puerto Escondido to be over.

CHAPTER SIXTEEN

Her name was Colette Cipriani, but everyone called her "Coco". Bob's first love. He had been smitten at first sight when he met her at a one of the Saturday night dances at the Horace Mann Girls School in New York. Coco was stunning, with her father, Carlo's, smooth olive skin, luxurious eyebrows, and dimpled chin and her mother, Francois', long wavy auburn hair, high cheekbones and sensuous lips. In repose or moving in lengthy strides, she projected an image that was both elegant and sexy. Though less voluptuous than the actress Sophia Loren, Coco resembled her enough to be taken for the screen star. So, it was no surprise that her looks and bearing and the way she moved got her lead roles in the School's Theater Club productions. Few would have guessed from her modest demeanor, though, that she had also been elected president of her class.

Though it may be displaced by another, there is nothing like a first love. And now that Coco's name and nearness has resurfaced,

Bob experiences a dimmed twinge of the heartache he had felt so long ago, when he lost her.

Memories of their youthful romance parade through his mind. He remembers, as a prep school senior, picking Coco up for a Saturday evening date at the Cipriani's in Manhattan. Their apartment was in The Langham at 135 Central Park West an old but, at that time, still prestigious building. Most of the furnishings of their small, high- ceilinged suite of rooms were a bricolage of fruitwood Italian provincial pieces (from Carlo's family), and carved/painted Louis XV reproductions (from Francois' family), most in need of some refurbishing. Bob especially remembers the creaky settee in the Cipriani's tiny foyer on which, after a date, he and Coco would make out, until a light under the door of her parents' bedroom signaled that the night's love-making was to be terminated.

When Bob had put aside enough from his weekly allowances, he would take Coco dancing in the Hotel Pennsylvania's Café Rouge, trying to arrive, if possible, in time to hear Glen Miller's big band open their first set with "Moonlight Serenade" and certainly in time to hear his and Coco's favorites, "In the Mood", "String of Pearls" and "Pennsylvania 6-500 and Tex Beneke's honking, tenor sax rendition of "Chattanooga Choo Choo." The best part of the evening for Bob, however, was slow dancing cheek-to-cheek with Coco as tenor Ray Eberle crooned love songs over the band's muted melodic backing.

Coco and he had also made the scene at the Astor Roof on Times Square to listen and dance to Tommy Dorsey's orchestra and Bob could still bring up the image of the diminutive trumpeter, Bunny Berrigan, spotlighted on the darkened dance floor, mesmerizing the audience with his inspired improvisation on Vernon Duke and Ira Gershwin's "I Can't Get Started."

On Coco's birthday, Bob had treated her to an evening in the stylish Persian Room at the Plaza to dance to Eddie Duchin's society orchestra. Between sets was a floor show featuring dancers, Tony and Sally De Marco. De Marco's ballroom dance routines were both elegant and electric. Tony, who had recently separated from his wife and longtime partner, Renee, had begun dancing with his new partner, Sally. The two were deeply in love, a feeling they projected in their dance routines, that evening. They were married shortly thereafter.

On their last date in New York, Coco had invited Bob to dinner at the New York Athletic Club where her father had recently been accepted as a member.

Sitting in the Club's 11th floor dining room, near a window overlooking Central Park and holding hands with Coco across the candle lit table, Bob was swept up in a tide of contentment. Alas however, high tides, whether in the sea or in life, last only too briefly.

Before long, they were off to college, Cocoa to Cornell, Bob to Yale. The eight-hour train and bus trip between New Haven and Ithaca made it impractical for them to see one another during that first semester and then, on December eighth war was declared on Japan and soon thereafter Bob signed up for a Marine Corps Officer Training Program which would enable him to continue college for two years and eight months, with no break, and then, after six months of satisfactory military service, receive his BA degree. Bob and Coco managed to stay in touch by letter and phone calls and, when, eventually he did get a week's leave, late in the fall, he made the trip to Ithaca, most of it in an unheated railroad coach. Even now Bob recalls the football game in Ithaca, cuddling with Coco in the Schoellkopf Field stands, cheering on Cornell's Big Reds as they demolished the Syracuse Orange 13-0, and later the two of them, dancing the night away at the Student Union. When they parted at the end of the weekend, Bob sensed that the banked fire of their romance had again burst into flame. But, after ten weeks of basic training at Paris Island and another ten weeks at Marine Corps Officers Training School in Quantico, he began to sense that their prolonged separation was depriving the fire of oxygen, allowing it to dwindle once more into smoldering embers.

Officers Training School in Quantico, Virginia, was physically and mentally grueling, a program designed by the Marine Corps to weed out those who might crack under the stress of combat.

Prospective officers were, however, provided a pressure relief valve in the form of weekend leaves. For most, that meant weekends in D.C. drinking, dancing, and for the more fortunate, sleeping with comely girls, some of whose boyfriends were already overseas. At first it was heady diversion but by the time Bob had begun his second ten weeks in Reserve Officers' School as a provisional Second Lieutenant, he realized that none of these brief liaisons were likely to flower into a deep, committed relationship for which he found himself longing.

His thoughts, his dreams kept returning to Coco. With Coco he could imagine tender love making, sharing life's joys and sorrows, victories and defeats. He longed to be with someone with whom he could share his innermost thoughts and feelings.

It would have been logical for Coco and Bob to have to waited out the war in the hope that they would be able to pick up their romance where it had left off. But Bob was concerned that their relationship might not survive the long separation. While he couldn't quite put his finger on it, he sensed, of late, that Coco had cooled slightly. What if she lost patience waiting for the war to end, a war that might grind on endlessly, and, impulsively, might take up with someone else? What if Coco decided she didn't want to get married, or what if he came back physically or mentally disabled, unable to provide for her? What if?

Misgivings and unanswerable questions dogged him in stressful, sleepless nights. Ultimately, the uncertainties became too stressful to bear and it was time to act.

"Drifted apart," the words Coco had chosen to explain to Lady Jane the end of her romantic involvement with Bob sounded like a cop-out to him. Either Coco, in retrospect, had found the memory of the separation too disturbing to think about or, more likely, having already revealed more information than she had intended to share with Jane, simply wanted to foreclose the conversation. This is what actually occurred.

Bob was about to graduate from Marine Reserve Officers School, receive his Second Lieutenant bars, and report for active duty with the Second Amphibious Tractor Battalion in Oceanside California. Feeling new self-esteem as a Marine Corps officer and having deep misgivings about leaving the East Coast without her, he called Coco from an outdoor telephone booth near the barracks.

"Coco, this is Second Lieutenant Rosenbaum calling."

"Oh, Bob, how wonderful. Congratulations."

"I have a ten-day leave coming up before my first assignment on the West Coast, but what I really wanted to say is that I am very much in love with you and I want to propose, to ask you, Coco, will you marry me? I think we could be very happy together." There was a brief silence before Coco replied. "Bob...I'm overwhelmed...and flattered " There was another pause." "This is so sudden and unexpected, Bob, I need some time to think this over. Can I call you back in a couple of days?" Bob shuddered but then told himself that her reaction was characteristic. Coco was one not to jump to important decisions, something he has always admired about her.

"Of course, sweetheart, but it is hard to reach me by phone on the base. Can I call you on Thursday around this time?"

"Certainly, and Bob, I feel really privileged that you have asked me."

"Till Thursday, then. I love you Coco." As Bob slowly put the handset back on the receiver and opened the phone booth door, a chilling gust of wind came up. On Thursday he was back in the same booth, dialing Coco's number.

"Coco, I could hardly wait to call you. Have you had enough time to think it over?"

"Yes, Bob, dear Bob, I have."

"And?"

"I've thought about it lot and I feel I'm not ready yet to make a permanent commitment, not now. I'm going to have to say no. I hope you understand." Bob's hand holding the receiver dropped and he leaned against the booth for support. He felt as if the wind has been knocked out of him, all his hopes dashed with the single word, 'no.' He raised the receiver again. It seemed to weigh ten pounds.

"Oh, Coco, I am so disappointed. Yes, I will try to understand."
He is struggling to continue. "Let me call you later when pull myself
together."

At first Coco wrote to him weekly, but with passing time the
frequency and warmth of her letters diminished. A natural
development, he wanted to believe, given the lengthening time since
they had been together. Or could it be that she taken up with
someone else? When Bob considered that possibility, it caused him
such angst that he tried to put it out of mind. Later, when he was
stationed on the island of Guam in the South Pacific his suspicion
was confirmed. A final letter arrived, in which Coco told him she
had decided to marry Frank Connolly, who had recently graduated
from Cornell's Medical School. Through a classmate he had run into
at his tenth Yale reunion, Bob learned that Conolly had interned at
Rutgers, completed a residence at St. Barnabus Medical Center, and
was building a lucrative private practice in Livingston, New Jersey.
The couple had moved from Livingston to Short Hills. Soon after
passing on this information to Bob, his classmate had moved to
Thailand so that was as much as Bob ever learned about Coco's life
until her name had resurfaced on Jane Dwight Sanders lips. And
now unaccountably Coco, who vanished from his life more than a
half century ago, has reappeared. It gets him speculating about how
different his life might have been if Coco had said yes to his
proposal. While he is sure life would have been less turbulent than

with Susie, he suspects that the early years with Coco might not have gone all that smoothly, given that both were high achievers and neither mature enough as young marrieds to have avoided adversarial competition instead of supportive partnership. When you are young and in love you don't see conflicts such as this coming. You are not aware of the seeds of character traits your loved one has brought along, which when watered and fertilized by the marriage grow into destructive, invasive plants. By the time he and Hildy had married, both were secure enough themselves to be able to nurture one another. Bob has to painfully remind himself, once more, that this latter part of his life is now defunct and that no amount of dwelling on it will bring it back.

Now, as Bob is about to leave Puerto Escondido for Oaxaca, he is determined to find Coco. Does she still have those qualities that made him fall in love with her in the first place? Is she still married to the interloper, Connolly.

CHAPTER SEVENTEEN

Back in Oaxaca at the apartment in Suites la Fe and feeling light headed from the fast five-thousand-foot elevation change from Puerto Escondido to Oaxaca, Bob collapses on the queen bed and promptly falls asleep. He is awakened nine hours later by the angry growling of cars and busses racing down the Avenida Juarez in front of his apartment. Refreshed by the sleep but famished, he walks up a few doors up Juarez to a tiny cafe attached to the Posada Yagul, where visiting friends on tight budgets have stayed. After downing an ice cream sundae-sized tumbler of fresh squeezed orange juice and consuming a plate of huevos rancheros, and sipping a cafe con leche, he ponders how he should go about locating Coco in Oaxaca.

Yesterday that project struck him as almost a mission impossible but now, after a good night's sleep and a hearty breakfast it seems somehow with some strategic thinking and a little luck, to be achievable.

"If this is the Connollys first time in Oaxaca," Bob reasons, "they are probably staying at one of the hotels in the old Historic

District. But which?" A good bet would be The Noria, nearby, the one Lady Jane had suggested to the Connollys while they were in Puerto Escondido.'

He walks south on Avenida Juarez and then west on Hidalgo to the Hostal La Noria. Though the walk is only three blocks and slightly downhill at that, Bob nevertheless has to stop twice to catch his breath.

"Not a good sign but maybe it's just the change in elevation" he tries to reassure himself as he reaches the front desk at the small Spanish Colonial hotel.

"Buenos dias, senor. Bienvenudos." says the desk clerk. Bob asks,

"Do you have a party of three by the name of Connolly staying here?" The clerk consults the computer screen on his desk.

"No, I don't see no Connolly?"

"Are you sure? They would have checked in last week."

"Momento, senor. Let me ask my associate." The clerk disappears, returns to the desk in a few moments.

"My associate, he says he remembers a party of three with the name Connolly. He remembers because he thought one of the women was really the Italian actress Sophia Loren. They registered, but the other woman, she didn't like her room, it was the only one we still had not occupado, so they left."

"Do you know where they went?"

"No. I am sorry, senor, no se," replies the clerk.

If the Connollys are not at the Noria, they could be at any of the hundred or so hotels in the Historic District. How to narrow down that formidable number? Where would he and Hildy have gone if there were no rooms at the Noria? A boutique hotel nearby, in easy walking distance to the Zocolo comes to Bob's mind, the Hotel de la Parra on Vincente Guerero.

But when he gets there, he is told that no one by the name of Connolly has registered recently. "O.K," he tells himself, "La Parra is not well known, a long shot." More likely they would have chosen or have been directed to one of the larger, better known hotels in the neighborhood. The Marques de Valle might be a good bet.

He walks slowly the few blocks to the seven-story plain vanilla pile at the north side of the Zocalo. The Marques de Valle he has been told, is owned by the family of a corrupt former governor of the State of Oaxaca. So, those who have been around Oaxaca for a while and in the know shun it. But uninitiated newcomers like the Connollys frequently stay there.

The desk clerk checks his register for Bob - no Connollys. He retreats to a sidewalk table outside the Italian Coffee Company at the corner, orders a latte and plots his next move. Perhaps Coco's sister-in-law rejected the Noria as insufficiently luxurious. Why hadn't he thought of that before? Could they be at the Camino Real, the luxuriously remodeled old convent up on Cinco de Mayo? Big bucks, from his perspective, but probably a good bet. Bob is not up to the four-block uphill climb to the luxury hotel, so he takes a taxi, drops into a large tan leather club chair in front of the Hotel's reception table, and asks the impeccably suited desk clerk if there

are any Connollys registered. The clerk's eyes light up. Yes, there is a party by that name. Would he like to speak with them on the house phone?

As he waits for the connection, Bob's heart beats faster as it did as a teen ager when he first spied Coco on the dance floor at the high school Saturday night dance.

"Hello." a male voice answers.

"Yes, hello. I am calling to speak to Coco Connolly. I am an old friend of hers."

"Ah ha, yes but my name is Connery and there is no one by the name of Coco here. Coco?"

"Sorry if I've inconvenienced you."

"Yes, well then…" The phone goes dead.

The three and a half blocks back to the Suites La Fe apartment is downhill, so Bob decides to walk it by way of Avenida Reforma. As he turns into Reforma, it strikes him that Casa de Las Bougambilias, an upscale B&B popular with Americans, might easily be where the

Connollys had ended up. Why hadn't he thought of that before?

At the rear of the garden-like patio, Bob finds the reception area but there is no one on duty. He rings the little bell on the counter and, slowly, a lanky, longhaired teenager appears, still watching a soccer game on his cell phone.

"Buenos dias, do you speak English?" asks Bob.

"A leetle"

"Do you have anyone by the name of Connolly staying here?"

"Como?"

"People by the name of Connolly – here I'll write the name for you." The teenager examines the writing.

"Si, si, Connolly. Dey are in rooms eight and nine.

"Can I talk to them on the house phone?".

"No!"

"Why not – porque no?"

"Dey are out." Bob excitedly scribbles a note to Coco, hands it to the young clerk.

"Could you give this to Colette Connolly, when she comes back?"

The clerk looks suspiciously at the note.

"It's O.K., I am a friend of hers. Amigo." The young man's face brightens.

"Ah you are friend. Un amigo. Entiendo, senor. He puts the note in the slot of the wooden box marked "9".

CHAPTER EIGHTEEN

The next morning at 11 AM, Bob's phone rings. He rushes to pick up.

"Coco?"

"Hola, Senor Rosenbaum?"

"That's me."

"Madelena will be in to clean the apartmento on Thursday, not today, jueves, no hoy, don't worry."

"Thank you." Bob, dejectedly, replaces the receiver on its base. *Well at least the phone works, he thinks. Could it be that I missed a call from Coco when I was out to dinner or earlier this morning when I was at the Colossus gym? Why didn't I leave my cell phone number on the note to Coco? Stupido. A more unsettling thought occurs. Maybe Coco didn't return the call because she isn't interested in seeing me again.*

At 4 PM, unable to contain himself any longer, he phones her at Bougambillias. Coco answers the phone. At the sound of her voice he suddenly feels weak and queasy, like a long-delayed aftershock of the sensation he experienced in a windy telephone booth a half a

century ago, when Coco had turned him down. He struggles to pull himself together, put himself in a more positive mood.

"Coco. Is it really you?"

"Bob, I'm so glad you called. I tried to reach you at the number you left, but there was no answer and no way to leave a message. What a coincidence—reconnecting—you and I—after what has it been? Over fifty years, and in Oaxaca of all places.

"It's good to hear your voice, Coco, how are you?"

"I'm well, Bob. Trying to put my life back together again—after Frank's death." Frank the interloper, finally out of the picture, thinks Bob, unconsciously experiencing a sense of relief and elation and then, consciously, a sense of guilt for having experienced them.

"Sorry, Coco, I didn't know."

"Yes, lung cancer – stage 3 by the time it was positively diagnosed. He went in 14 months—after a lot of suffering. And you, Bob, how are you? Are you married?" Bob replies but with all the energy is sucked out of his voice by what he has to say

"No," Hildy, my wife, you never met her, was killed in an automobile accident almost a year ago, now. I'm still not over it." No I'm not over it, but I've got to get over it, he thinks, and I don't need to burden Coco with Hildy's death, certainly not now.

"How awful."

"Yes, awful, but life goes on" There is a long pause in which Bob senses that if he does not change the direction of the conversation now, his opportunity to reconnect with Coco may slip away. He strikes a positive note, "Coco, I'd love to see you –catch up on all those years – if that's even possible. Could we meet for dinner tonight?"

"I'd like that, Bob. Can you wait a minute. I want to check with my sister and brother-in-law. I'm traveling with them. Suspect they'd be delighted to have an evening to themselves. Can you hold the phone?"

"Of course." The phone goes dead for a couple of minutes.

"Hello, Bob, Are you still there? Good. Yes, I can meet you for dinner." Bob feels a sense of relief and elation. "Did you have a place in mind?"

"I was thinking of La Biznaga," He says in happy anticipation.

"Have you been there?"

"No, but I've heard its good."

"O.K. La Biznaga it is. Shall I pick you up?"

"Is it far from here?"

"About five blocks."

"Then I'll meet you there. The walk will do me good. How do I find it?"

"Know where the Santo Domingo Church is?"

"Yes."

"There's a block-long pedestrian street at the corner called Allende. If you walk up Allende you'll come to Garcia Vigil. Turn right on Garcia Vigil. Biznaga is about a half a block up, on your right."

"I think I've got it. What time?"

"Seven?"

"Seven it is fine"

"Can't wait to see you, Coco." Bob experiences a new high, the kind he has not felt for a long time. But, almost at once, it begins to nibbled away by fear. Will Coco be disappointed by how he has aged and how his recent life experience has eaten away at his self-confidence and joi de vivre?

Bob figures that, because of his breathlessness, that there is no way he can walk the six blocks, mostly uphill, so he hails a cab at his corner and arrives at the restaurant a few minutes before seven. At five past seven there is no sign of Coco, and remembering that she was always prompt, he begins to worry. Did she get cold feet? Is she going to stand me up? Bob suddenly finds himself in a sweat. He feels as nervous as a schoolboy on his first date. "Ridiculous," he tells himself. 'After all I've been through?—Marine Officer in two wars, losing two sons and a spouse. Get ahold of yourself, man. Buck up!'

At that moment Coco saunters into the room and he is dumbstruck. The long wavy auburn hair he remembers is now white and cut fashionably short. There are fine wrinkles and feint circles under her eyes, but they are not discernable in the dimly lit courtyard. Coco is wearing a black designer sheath that few women over fifty have the figure to wear, but Coco with her thin, muscular body, pulls it off stunningly.

"Bob." She gives him a peck on the cheek. "How good to see you again - after so many years. You're looking well, not as young as I remember you but – more handsome. The harder features and a few lines are becoming."

"And you, Coco, what can I say–dazzling–of course you always have been." They are seated in the old stone-paved patio, near a large exotic tree which is its centerpiece. The waiter arrives to take their drink order.

"Coco, what would you like to drink? I'd guess by now, you have graduated from the claret lemonades of our salad days."

She giggles. "What are you having, Bob?"

"I'm going for a Margarita. They are famous here for their Margaritas, generous and not too sweet, not too sour."

"I usually have a glass of white wine, but a Margarita sounds adventurous. I'll have one too."

"Salt on the rim?"

"Sure. But now fill me in on what you've been up to over the past fifty years. After the war. You got married?" Bob reflects momentarily. "Yes, not a happy marriage, but Susy and I had four children, all boys, and somehow we managed to stay together—for over thirty years."

"And what kind of work did you do? Bob fills in Coco on his life since they had last spoken. Bob pauses, realizing the rush of conflicting emotions he is feeling while fast-forwarding his past.

"And yourself, Coco. How about you?"

"Yes, so Frank, you may not remember, was a medical student at Cornell when we met. We got married after I graduated. I worked as stage manager for a theater company. Frank interned at Rutgers, did his residency at St. Barnabas, set up practice in Livingston. We had three children, Una, Chip, and Clarissa. As I told you, Frank died - fourteen months ago now, of lung cancer. It was horrible."

"I can imagine. And was yours a happy marriage?" asks Bob, wondering whether Coco's marriage had been contented like his own to Hildy or troubled like first marriage to Linda. Coco replied unhesitatingly.

"Unhappy. From the beginning I don't think I was much in love with Frank, but my mother was promoting him, heavily. Mother was a social climber and, not having climbed the social ladder as far as she hoped, was trying to realize her ambitions in me. Mother convinced me that Frank had good prospects. She was impressed that he was on his way to becoming a doctor and that his family was socially prominent." Coco takes a sip of her Margarita which he has just set down and cocks her head at Bob. "I don't know if I should

tell you this?"

"What?"

"Well, mother discouraged me so far as you were concerned. She thought you were not suitable husband material, and afraid you might not come back from the war – and that even if you did that your family didn't have acceptable social connections. She never said as much, but I suspect she was anti-Semitic."

"So, I had two strikes against me from the get-go?"

"I should have listened to my heart, then, instead of being persuaded by mother - but you know how it is – when you are young – and insecure, and easily influenced." Bob shakes his head involuntarily, believing yet not wanting to believe.

"I'm glad you've told me, even at this late date. I can still remember, Coco, your words when I proposed from that windy telephone booth in Quantico – you said you were "overwhelmed - overwhelmed and flattered" but that you needed "some time to think it over." At the time I didn't understand – understand why you were conflicted. Now I do, I understand. Coco, this may sound crazy, but it's still painful. Why should it be? Tell me. What difference does it make anymore?"

"You're right, Bob, it's water, long over the dam. I guess, at the time, I was just trying to tell you, awkwardly – that though I was not going to marry you that I, nevertheless did love you." Both Coco and Bob are caught up in the moment, she having blurted out the long suppressed, bittersweet truth, he for being unable to take any comfort in what she has just told him. He hurries to change the subject feeling that Coco should, at the time, have had the courage to reject her mother's narrow- minded opposition.

After they have ordered dinner she asks if he is retired and he tells her that he is but keeps himself between newspaper writing, volunteering, tennis, bicycling, sailing and socializing, none of which completely relieve his feelings of loneliness. Then he asks,

"And you, Coco – how've you been faring since Frank died?"

"Not well. You see, that last year when Frank was so ill–I was spending almost all of my time as his caretaker. Our social life, my other interests – everything was put on hold. By the time Frank died, I was so wrung out that I just felt like curling up in a ball and shutting out the rest of the world. It's only been in the past few months that I've mustered up the will and energy to try to pull my life together again." Coco tears up "I was exhausted, so completely exhausted." She turns away, dries her eyes on her napkin. "Sorry."

Bob reaches across the table and puts his hand on hers. She looks up, then slowly withdraws her hand and says, "It's not you, Bob. Got nothing to do with you. It's just that I'm just not ready. Still grieving, not for Frank, heaven knows–for myself, I guess…

Let's talk about something else. That tree in the center of the courtyard, its trunk seems to be covered with what looks like thorns–

I've never seen a tree anything like it. What is it?"

"They are thorns. Colloquially, it's known as the Marriage Tree – because it's thorny, like some marriages."

"I can identify with that.'

"Want to elaborate?" Coco looks away. "No, no I don't. Not now." They pick their way through dinner, neither fully able to enjoy the outstanding Mexican cuisine

"How about some desert, coffee?" asks Bob. Coco considers for a moment, then replies,

"Think I'll pass. I need to get back to the posada and get some sleep. Didn't sleep much last night. Bob, I'm sorry to be such a spoil sport." Bob feels the whole evening has been a bust and wonders if he could have handled it differently.

As they walk out onto the sidewalk, Coco says, "It's only a few blocks to the Bougambillias – think I'll walk. It will do me good."

"Mind if I walk with you?"

"I'd like that – I'm really sorry I've been in such a bitchy mood tonight."

He takes her hand, which she accepts, and they stroll the few blocks down to the posada, hardly exchanging a word.

When they arrive, Coco turns to Bob and says,

"You seem to be breathing hard – are you O.K.?"

Before answering he considers, then decides it is too late in the evening and too early in their renewed relationship to explain in detail the cause of his breathing difficulty.

"Yes, well, I don't do well at high elevations."

She lets it drop at that.

Soon they arrive at Bougambillias. Coco turns to Bob. "I'm going to say goodbye here. It was wonderful to see you."

He looks at her quizzically.

"No, I really mean it - and I loved the restaurant." She pauses momentarily before adding, "And I am sorry I fouled up the evening." She puts her hand on his shoulder and kisses him lightly on the cheek.

"Can I see you again?" he asks.

"Yes, yes, of course. I'd like you to meet my in-laws. Let me see what their plans are and give you a ring in the morning." As Bob strolls slowly back to his diggs thoughts about a developing relationship with Coco crowd in. He is encouraged that the strong physical and mental attraction between them has remained, undiminished by time and their life experiences but he worries that the noxious emotional baggage Coco may be carrying from her marriage to Frank could spill out to poison their own relationship. And he is apprehensive about Coco's strength of character because of what she has just revealed as her reasons for marrying Frank. At a critical turn in Bob's progressive decline in the foreseeable future, he questions, would Coco simply jump ship and abandon him?

CHAPTER NINETEEN

The next morning, Coco calls to invite him to dinner that evening to meet her in-laws. He arrives five minutes early at La Olla, the restaurant that is part of Bougambillias, their B&B. While he normally avoids arriving earlier than invited, feeling it puts his hosts in an awkward position, he is tonight, more concerned about arriving after them, panting from the mild exertion of walking the three blocks from his apartment to the restaurant. He has yet to reveal his progressive amyloidosis to Coco, and he certainly wants to avoid it now with her in-laws present.

He arrives not a moment too soon. Just as his breathing is returning to normal, they arrive, Coco, her brother-in-law, Graydon Connolly and his wife, Dorothy. Coco plants a reassuring kiss on Bob's cheek and makes the introductions. Dorothy immediately proposes that they eat in Olla's upstairs dining room. Bob, demurs. He prefers the lively street-level dining room with its typical mix of Mexican locals and tourists. He dislikes the upstairs dining room which has been outlandishly decorated in pink and yellow by a flamboyant decorator friend of the owner and because it is almost exclusively occupied by American tourists, who seem to feel more secure when surrounded by their own.

No sooner is the foursome seated than Dorothy begins babbling. She and Graydon had visited Monte Alban, the Pre-Columbian archeological site above Oaxaca, that morning. It was awesome, just awesome! Imagine them building – all those temples," Dorothy throws her arms into the air, "a whole city like that – thousands of years ago on top of a mountain, without," she gasps for breath, "without tractors–and this afternoon, I found this wonderful native craft shop and..." Coco looks at Bob and rolls her eyes. Bob, amused at Dorothy's motor-mouth behavior, cocks his head and smiles in acknowledgement, shifts his gaze to Graydon, Coco's deceased husband's narrow shouldered brother, a Brooks Brothers classic cut type. Graham, as soon as he gets a chance to put in a word, establishes his own bona fides by revealing that he has recently retired after 30 years as a Private Client Account Manager at U.S. Trust. Almost immediately Graydon starts questioning Bob as to where he was born and bred, his school, college and fraternal affiliations, where he worked and where he lives now. Bob answers Graydon's questions, trying to conceal his annoyance at being grilled by what he has sized up as a mid-level corporate pencil pusher probing to decide if he, Bob, is a socially acceptable companion for his sister-in-law. Bob recognizes he is becoming irritated. Coco who has become aware of her brother-in-law's pointed questioning, looks over at Bob, shrugs her shoulders and silently mouths the word, sorry.

As far as Bob is concerned, the only positive attributes of the evening aside from looking at Coco's lovely face and exchange an occasional word with her when Dorothy pauses to catch her breath, is La Olla's chicken mole prepared with a rich, spicy sauce, and their pastel de chocolate, unquestionably one of the best in Oaxaca.

The following day is Sunday, Coco's last before flying home. Bob has invited her to the Oaxaca State Band concert at noon in the Zocalo and later to dinner at his favorite restaurant. On his slow walk back to his apartment Bob is troubled at Graydon's seemingly antagonistic attitude to his taking up with Coco. Is Graydon trying to throw a monkey wrench into Coco and his long dormant but reviving romance? He shakes off the thought. No, he vows, this no-account social snob is not going to get between him and Coco. No way. Bob has run into these types before. More bark than bite. Bob will deal with Graydon in due time. Meanwhile, there is the prospect of tomorrow with Coco. His spirits rise.

CHAPTER TWENTY

When Bob arrives at the corner of the Zocalo, near the Cathedral where the concert is to take place, many of the folding chairs in rows facing the band are already occupied. Bob finds a couple of empty ones in the shade of a huge arching Indian Laurel tree, sits down in one, and puts his straw sombrero on the other. Coco arrives momentarily, dressed in a red and white embroidered Mexican blouse and a flowing navy cotton baize skirt. Bob rises to greet her.

"You've gone native." He smiles, first holding her at arm's length, looking her over approvingly, then drawing her near and kissing her tenderly. She blushes but does not pull away.

Members of the Oaxaca State Band, in white shirts and black trousers, begin to drop into place like pieces of a jigsaw puzzle: saxophones, clarinets, oboes and flutes surrounded by kettle drums, trumpets and trombones, gleaming nickel mellophones and polished brass tubas until the picture puzzle is complete.

A stumpy Elisio Martinez Garcia mounts the plywood conductor's podium and, smiling at the audience, bows stiffly. Martinez looks clownish, his large head emerging from a black serge jacket extending halfway down his thighs and his trousers, breaking so far over his shoes that he seems in danger of tripping on them. But when Martinez raises his baton and begins to conduct a stirring Sousa march, his droll appearance is forgotten as the audience soon becomes mesmerized by his exceptional command and musicianship.

The pot pouri program of familiar compositions has been designed to please everyone. Dvořak's Symphony No. 9 followed by Strauss' Blue Danube Waltz, an excerpt from Beethoven's Symphony No. 5. Then, after a brief intermission, comes the Mexican composer Carlos Chavez' Simphonia India followed by Offenbach's Barcarolle. At this point the orchestra breaks into a Paso Doble, and several well-dressed, elderly Mexican couples leave their seats to dance to it. One feels as if transported back into the Mexico of the thirties. The final offering is Mexican composer/singer Alvaro Carrillo's haunting ballad, 'Sabor a Mi" sung by a grey-haired tenor.

After the song is over Coco clasps her hands and exclaims, "How beautiful. Do you know what the Spanish words mean?"

Bob nods affirmatively, his eyes tearing up with an overwhelming feeling of joy at being reunited with Coco after so long.

"It translates something like this –

For so long we have delighted in this love
Our souls are drawn together, oh so close
That I keep the taste of you
But you also hold within
A taste of me"

"That is so heartfelt, so romantic."

Bob grasps Coco's hands and squeezes them gently, and looking into her eyes, says "yes, romantic and bittersweet because, for so long, so long, you and I, we have been unable to 'delight in this love' – the love I feel for you."

"And, Bob, the love I feel for you – and yet…"

"And yet?" Bob is confused. Why, at a moment like this is Coco hesitating?

"The love I feel, all my emotions, are imprisoned and I don't know how to escape with them to be able to give my love to anyone. Maybe never. Does that sound crazy?" Bob, who feels he can unconditionally give his love to Coco is having a hard time understanding her quandary but wants to acknowledge and understand it.

"No, no it doesn't, but it could be that you are recovering from a serious injury and just need more time to heal."

Coco considers. "I sort of understand that the emotional imprisonment I'm feeling is a defensive mechanism to protect myself against being hurt again – and I realize it didn't start with Frank's illness. It began long before then, early in our marriage, and when Frank died I figured I would recover. When I didn't, I went to see a psychiatrist.

"Did that help?"

"It might have, if he hadn't turned out to be a creep, and a womanizer."

"Where were you living at that time?"

"I had to get out of the New Jersey house - too many unhappy memories there, so I went to stay with Graydon and Dorothy in Hingham, Massachusetts." Bob tries but cannot suppress a giggle.

Coco looks annoyed. "What's the matter, I don't think I said anything funny."

Bob tries to regain control of himself. "No, it's nothing you said, but I think I'm on to something—I know this is a long shot but let me take a guess."

"About what?"

"The name of the psychiatrist. Was his name Ransahoff, Gregory Ransahoff?" Coco's jaw drops.

"How could you know? Are you some kind of a clairvoyant?

Coco frowns. "Anyway, I don't see what's so funny."

"You my," says Bob. You see, I was being seen by Ransahoff at the same time. While I was in the waiting room I saw an attractive woman whom I thought looked familiar, storm out of the office. I tried to get her name, but the receptionist refused to give it to me. It was you!"

"Oh, no." Coco looks disbelievingly at Bob and then they both break into unrestrained laughter which relieves, momentarily, the stress that has been building up in their relationship.

"That felt good," he says.

"Yes, didn't it." Coco manages, wiping tears of laughter from her eyes as Bob proposes

"Let's meet for dinner, later. Have you been to Restaurante Catédral? Asks Bob.

"No, never heard of it."

"It's my favorite in Oaxaca, just a block and a half north of the Cathedral behind us. Shall we meet there at seven?"

CHAPTER TWENTY-ONE

Coco is seated on the antique Spanish Colonial bench in the arch-ceilinged

entrance of Catédral as Bob arrives. His shortness of breath has made it take longer than he estimated to walk to the restaurant.

Recognizing Bob, Cathédral's elderly head waiter breaks into a broad smile.

"Bienvenido senor, que buenoverte de nuevo" (how good to see you again). Bob grasps the headwaiter's bony hand but is unable to summon up a suitable Spanish phrase to express how glad he is to see the man again, so he settles, weakly, for "Igualmente." ("Likewise") being all he can muster.

The waiter leads them across the dimly lit patio to a small linen-covered, candle-lit table near a small fountain of carved Cantera, the pale green volcanic rock that embellishes the facades of Oaxaca's historic buildings.

"Margarita?" asks Bob.

"Are they as good as those at Biznaga?" asks Coco.

"That's a tall order–they're a bit tarter, but delicious."

"O.K. a Margarita it is." While they are waiting for their drinks a waiter arrives with an 'amuse bouche', a tiny cheese filled puff pastry topped with guacamole and red pepper. Bob and Coco inspect the menu and order.

After the waiter has left, Coco turns to Bob, cocks her head slightly and muses, "what a coincidence, our both seeing Ransahoff, the psychiatrist, and at the same time."

"Yes, extraordinary. But coincidences like this do happen and more often than you'd expect." Bob wonders if both this chance encounter and then the conversation about Coco with Jane Dwight-Sanders were coincidences or some mysterious manifestation of fate.

Coco returns to her theme. "Ransahoff. Such a lech - and a fraud!"

Bob reflects. "Maybe not such a fraud. He was able to get me to face up."

"Face up to what, Bob?"

"To the fact that if I wanted to come out of depression, I would have to stop brooding about the past and stop feeling sorry for myself – and that I'd have to muster the energy to begin living positively again and to stop worrying every night about the next day."

"That's a tough assignment. Have you been able to do all that?"

Bob thinks how he is going to frame his reply so it won't discourage Coco from finding a way out of her own emotional dilemma.

"Honestly, it's been a hell of a struggle. At first, I'd get up one morning feeling like my old self, do something useful and feel a sense of accomplishment. But the next day, I'd be so down that I could hardly get out of bed–life didn't seem worth living."

"But now, now you're feeling better?"

"Yes, gradually I've been able to reconnect with friends, and, I've started writing my newspaper column again, but, most important, I have found you. I see the possibility of love, of our being together again after all these years. It warms my heart–gives me hope."

"I feel that way too, Bob, but as I've told you, something is holding me back, something which makes me afraid to trust my own feelings. My marriage to Frank, it really did a number on me. Felt as if I was living on top of a land mine with Frank holding the detonator and threatening to ignite it at any moment if things did not go his way. I understand now that he was using affection as a tool to control me and the children. As long as we did his biding, he would dole out morsels of affection to us, but if we crossed him in any way, he would quickly snatch them away."

Bob considers. "And couldn't you just have simply called him out on that kind of bullying?"

Coco reflects. "I know it sounds as though I was a wimp and that I should have been able to stand up to Frank, but, believe me, once you get sucked into that kind of a relationship you begin to blame yourself for whatever goes wrong and you lose your confidence in your own judgment. That's why I'm afraid now, afraid of exposing myself to another destructive relationship. It would be too painful. Having made such a terrible mistake once, I find I can't trust my feelings now.

"But, Coco, didn't you sense this problem with Frank from the get-go?"

"No, because our relationship didn't start out that way. He was sexy. Good looking. Women were drawn to him and he was attracted to them, especially me, and that was very flattering. But, Frank must have had a weak ego and as time went on, his way of bolstering his self-esteem was to put down those around him, especially me and the children. I realize I should have left Frank years ago, but I rationalized that it would be better to wait until the children had grown up. But then when they had, I felt too insecure myself to make the move. And then Fank became ill and I felt I couldn't abandon him. And all of it has caused me to build up this protective wall to keep myself from being injured again.

Bob is deeply distressed at Coco's revelation and gasps for words to express his commiseration. "Oh, Coco, I am so sorry that you have had to endure all this. It all seems so unfair."

She attempts a smile but tears well up. She dabs her eyes with her table napkin. "Oh, my, Bob. I thought this was going to be such a joyful evening and now I've gone and spoiled it for you." Bob sighs, relieved to understand that her unresponsiveness is not a personal rejection but at the same time he is apprehensive, wondering if Coco will be able to free herself of the emotional baggage she is carrying

"No, you haven't spoiled it," he reassures her. I'm glad you've let me in on what's been going on. I'm feeling better, now that I understand that your coolness has to do with what you have been through and not your feelings about me."

"Bob, you are a dear to be so understanding."

"Coco, be patient with yourself. It is going to take time. I know. Others can be supportive, but they can't do the heavy lifting. We have to do it, ourselves. One thing you can count on-."

"Yes?"

"I am willing to wait. We've traveled different paths, you and I, and they have kept us apart—for much of our lives. So, I'd be willing to wait some more, years more, if it weren't for..."

Bob hesitates, realizing that, depending on how fast his disease progresses, he may not be able to wait very long.

"If it weren't for?" Bob clears his throat. "Remember when you said that I seemed out of breath the other evening? And I said it was the altitude."

"Yes."

"Well it wasn't just the altitude. There's a physical reason for my breathlessness."

"Don't be silly, Bob. You're the picture of health. You are as trim and fit as most men in their sixties.

"Unfortunately, I'm not in good shape."

"You're exaggerating."

"No, a cardiologist in Boston who knows his stuff has concluded that I am suffering from amyloidosis.'

"What's that?"

"Well, it's not good. It's a disease which makes it hard for you to breathe when you exert yourself. And it's progressive—gets worse as time goes on."

"But, Bob, surely they can treat that."

"Maybe yes, maybe no. I have to go back for more tests at the end of the month when I get home."

"And does this disease progress slowly?"

"Sometimes slowly, sometimes rapidly. I'll know more after the tests. For now, why don't we shelve the subject?" Coco, who is emotionally spent, readily agrees, but Bob is now beset by doubts about how Coco will react to his own disclosure, once it sinks in. Having experienced the burden of caring for someone declining, with an incurable disease, would she, even if she loved him, be willing to become involved?

CHAPTER TWENTY-TWO

Back home in Kingston, Bob tries to ignore his poorly functioning heart which is like a nagging child, demanding constant attention. After finishing his routine loop walk around the neighborhood, he senses he is more out of breath and tired than normal – or, he questions, is he just imagining this?

Dr. Hawk has had him undergo a new echocardiogram and another blood test before this, his three-month follow-up appointment.

"How are you feeling?" the cardiologist asks taking a seat at the small desk in the examining room.

Bob, while anxious about what he thinks may be a change for the worse in his condition is relieved to be able to unburden himself to his physician. "Well, taking my regular walk around the neighborhood, yesterday, I seemed to be more out of breath and more tired than before. But, maybe I was just imagining that."

Hawk, leans forward, toggles the images on the monitor back and forth several times, and swivels around. "No, it's not your imagination. The tests do show a small functional decline, but it's so minor that I'm surprised you felt it so noticeably."

Bob hears functional decline and figures the rest is just window dressing.

"Not good news?" he asks.

Hawk gives Bob a reassuring look. "Nothing to be alarmed about. I'm going to increase your medication dosage slightly, which may help. I could arrange for you to get a little supplementary oxygen to help relieve your symptoms." Bob panics. The suggestion of oxygen brings up the image of the frail elderly man Bob encountered a couple of days previously hunched over on a mobility scooter with a large oxygen tank with gauges, cautiously maneuvering the aisles of the local Walmart.

He frets, Is this my future. "Are you suggesting that I should be walking around with tubes in my nose carrying an oxygen tank?"

"No, but before you're about to exert yourself, say taking a walk or whenever you're feeling especially short of breath, a few minutes of oxygen may help make breathing easier."

Bob considers but rejects the whole idea as incompatible with his mind's eye vision of trips to exotic islands and riverboat cruises with Coco.

He fends off further discussion with, "I'll think about it."

Hawk continues, "Before further treatment I think we need a positive confirmation of the diagnosis, which we can make with another simple test which I can arrange for you to take today before you leave the hospital, if that's agreeable?"

Bob thinks for a moment, *What's to be lost, and maybe there's a slim chance that the diagnosis was wrong.* He quickly agrees,

"Sure, let's get it over with."

When something we face in life is fearsome enough, we often get into a conversation about it with ourselves. It is a way of creating enough detachment from an upsetting situation to be able to deal with it more objectively. On the drive home, Bob is having such a conversation with himself, about his perceived physical decline and its effect on his developing relationship with Coco.

"It would be fulfilling," he tells himself, to live with Coco—if she was willing. In addition to physical closeness, there would be so many things we could enjoy together, at least for a time. Bike trips abroad might no longer be in the cards, but we could travel—to Mexico where we could rent a small house by the sea, or, we might take a cruise'. 'The idea of cruise ships has never appealed to me, but who knows if I'm no longer to get around easily, cruising will still be doable and with Coco, it could be fun.'

Arriving back home he feels exhausted. It has been a physically and emotionally draining day.

Bob plops down on his bed and sleeps soundly for two hours. When he wakens he is back to thinking again about Coco, realizing that so far his thoughts have been only from his own perspective and not from Coco's.

He sees that Frank's death has finally enabled Coco to escape a debilitating marriage and now, now that she's nearly ready to escape, to fly, could he be about to clip her wings. "As you continue to fail," he tells himself, "her life as your care giver, will become ever more restricted, caging her once again. Under such circumstances wouldn't her love and compassion for you only sour into regret and resentment?" Staying together could turn into a cancer which would metastisize, consuming both of us, he concludes. Separation now will be painful, he thinks, but, in the end, Coco will recover and thrive. For her sake, for both our sakes, Bob tells himself, the right thing to do is to end our relationship before it destroys both of our lives. I must get Coco to see this.

Bob tells himself this is the time to call her. Then he hears another voice, telling him to hold off until he sees Hawk again and gets the definitive test results. Possibly, he doesn't have amyloidosis at all, but something else less serious and curable. Not likely, he acknowledges but, still, a possibility. A slim candle of hope flickers.

CHAPTER TWENTY-THREE

It is early morning. Having undergone the further test procedure, Bob is back at Brigham & Women's in the same consulting room on the same cold aluminum chair, awaiting Hawk. He picks at his thumb cuticle. Will the new test have identified a cause of his breathlessness other than amyloidosis, a condition that is treatable and will enable him to renew his lease on life? The wait seems interminable. Finally, Hawk enters the room, greets Bob and sits down in front of the monitor.

"So what have you found, Doctor?"

Hawk pauses, then looks up. "Bob, I've examined the new test results and, as I suspected they would, they confirm a positive diagnosis of amyloidosis of the heart wall." Bob slumps, feeling hopeless and completely spent, like a man hoping for an acquittal for a crime he did not commit who has just received a death sentence.

Henry Hawk assumes his most reassuring mien. "The good news is that it doesn't seem to have spread to other organs, the liver or kidneys, so chemotherapy is an option."

Bob sighs, feeling as though his death sentence has been changed to a short, miserable life sentence, responds in a tone of bitter resignation, "Well, bully for that. But, from what I've read online, the average survival rate for amyloidosis of the heart is thirteen months without treatment− seventeen months with treatment. Is that correct?"

"That data is probably not from the most recent studies. I think we're doing better than that. And, you know, Bob, it's a good idea not to pay too much attention to averages."

"Meaning?"

"Your amyloidosis seems to be progressing slowly and you are in exceptionally good physical condition otherwise. There's a good chance you'll live two, three, even four years."

"Without chemotherapy?"

"Bob, these things are impossible to predict, every individual is different, but that's a likely possibility."

"And with chemo?"

"In your case, who knows, a year longer, maybe several." Bob feels despair at how short a reprieve chemotherapy will provide and suddenly nauseous as he thinks about its side effects.

"My sister-in-law underwent chemotherapy for cancer last year and it made her so sick that she decided to discontinue the treatments."

"Yes, well, people react differently. There can be bad side effects, but we have ways of controlling them. We can start you on palliative care now and I'd recommend you consider chemotherapy."

"I'm going to have to think about that." Bob weighs the short life extension chemotherapy could provide against its nauseating and debilitating side effects. He concludes it's a heads I lose, tails you win coin toss.

Hawk continues, "Of course. I want to follow up with you in three weeks to see if the medication I prescribed the other day is providing you some relief and if you tolerate it well. We can discuss chemotherapy again, then"

Bob gets back to the house in Kingston a little after 1 PM, has prepared himself a sandwich and is munching it despondently when the phone rings.

"Coco!"

"Yes, Bob, it's me. I hadn't heard from you for a few days so I began to worry. I was wondering how the tests came out?"

Bob hesitates a moment, trying to think how best to word his answer.

"Bob?"

"Sorry, well, the tests were not encouraging. They confirmed that it's a condition of the heart wall called amyloidosis that's causing my breathlessness."

"But its treatable, right?"

"Partially. It's complicated," he replies quietly.

"Bob, I was planning to come up to Massachusetts this weekend to visit the in-laws, Dorothy and Frank. Any chance we could get together?"

Bobs voice brightens as he is caught up in the happy prospect of being with Coco and her eagerness to be with him. "Coco, that would be wonderful. I'd love to show you the house, and we can discuss this medical stuff. Why don't you come down Saturday around five? There will still be enough light to enjoy the view over drinks here and then go out to dinner."

"Sounds perfect. I'd love to. And, Bob…"

"Yes?"

"Don't worry about yourself about your condition. I'm sure you're going to be OK."

Bob feels a relief valve opening and releasing the pressure brought on by worry about his condition and uncertainty about Coco's feelings towards him. "I love you, Coco," he says gratefully.

"That will keep me content until Saturday."

CHAPTER TWENTY-FOUR

It is 4 PM on Saturday and Bob is still tidying up the house in anticipation of Coco's arrival. As he tosses a dirty shirt into the big woven Oaxaca basket that serves as a laundry hamper, he glances over at the shrine to Hildy on the bedside table. Past time to dismantle it, he decides. It would be embarrassing if Coco were to see it, after all his brave talk at dinner about having moved on with his life.

When Coco arrives, the sun is low in the sky, rendering the weathered cedar exterior of the house in an apricot glow. Bob and Coco exchange a polite kiss at the front door, hardly the long, langourous kiss Bob feels would express his longing for her. He hangs up her coat and she strides into the open, high-ceilinged living room. The east side of the house, a continuous expanse of sliding glass, looks over a broad deck to the sun-dappled bay beyond. The sun highlights Clark's Island in the bay and Bug Light, the distant lighthouse, in a flattering orange hue.

"Breathtaking!" Coco exclaims. "What an extraordinary house. How did you ever find this place?"

"Truth be told, we didn't. Had to build it. I found this waterfront lot with a shack on it and these huge trees—and decided to build. The view was great but the neighborhood was, still is, a little funky.

"Now that you mention it, when I got close, I did wonder if I was in the wrong place."

"How about a drink?"

"Sure, what are you offering, do you have white wine?"

"I do. I also looked up the recipe for Margaritas, online. I could fix a couple for us if you'd prefer."

"Gee, haven't had a Margarita since our dinner in Oaxaca. But isn't it a lot of trouble."

"No, it will only take a few minutes. If they turn out to be unfit for human consumption we can always switch to white wine. While I'm fixing the drinks why don't you take a stroll around the house?"

By the time Coco gets back to the bar Bob is pouring Margaritas into two thick green rimmed Oaxacan glasses and hands one to Coco.

"Salud!"

"Gracias. They sure look authentic, right down to the salt on the rim. Bob, this house is fabulous. Who designed it?

"You know, Coco, most of my career has been working with architectural systems and construction so some of the design ideas are ones I've picked up along the way. But, as you can imagine, it it takes a skilled architect to take ideas and incorporate them into a workable building design and, luckily, I knew one, Hildy's younger brother."

"The design looks mid-century, Bauhaus, something Mies van der Rohe

might have designed." Bob chuckles.

Coco looks perplexed. "Did I say something funny?"

"Sort of. You see, when the house was finished a few years ago, my friends kept

bugging me to give it a name it and the one I came up with was 'Ode to Mies.' And, your house in Short Hills – are you happy with it?" asks Bob.

"As soon as I stepped in the door after I got back from Mexico, I realized that the

house was much too big for me alone – With the kids gone, it didn't make any sense.

I've decided to put it on the market. Been cleaning out for weeks. You wouldn't believe the

amount of stuff you accumulate in a half century."

"And, when you sell, where will you go?"

"Graydon and Dorothy want me to move up here to Massachusetts – but I'm resisting.

Outside of them, I don't know a soul in Massachusetts – and I'd be leaving a lot of old friends in

Short Hills, so, I've been looking at a couple of condos there. Actually saw one I liked a lot – but it's expensive. Now that's all up in the air."

"You wouldn't be a stranger here. You'd know me and my friends would love you."

"Yes, and that makes it more complicated. But as I told you, I'm not ready yet to commit to another relationship" Coco sighs. "Maybe, I'll never be." Bob grimaces, feeling rejected yet powerless to change Coco's feelings.

"Living in Short Hills," Coco continues, "and seeing you when I can – maybe that makes more sense for the time being."

Bob senses this could be the moment to tell Coco more about his own diagnosis and broach the subject of a permanent separation with her, but just as he is putting his thoughts together, Coco picks up a copy of *"The Da Vinci Code"* from atop the oak map cabinet coffee table.

"Everyone's talking about this book," she says. "I just started it a couple of days ago. A real page turner. What do you think of it?"

"Well, it's certainly well written, keeps you engaged, but the plot's too implausible for me. The premise of a Priory of Scion and the secret location of the vastly important

religious relic, all that is too much of a stretch for me. I guess I'm a stick in the mud realist."

When they finish their drinks, Bob says, "There's a pretty good restaurant near here in Kingston. It's called Solstice. I'll drive so you can leave your car here and pick it up at the house after dinner. The snow is falling as they get into Bob's car. The restaurant, formerly the local railroad station. retains its original yellow brick and timber exterior and its interior tiled walls and floors. To create a welcoming dining space the hard surfaces have been softened with carpeting and parchment shaded light fixtures that bathe the linen covered tables and upholstered chairs in a soft glow. Coco seems delighted.

After they have ordered, Bob reaches across the table, taking Coco's hand in his and looking into her eyes, says, "seems to me we've been talking mostly about architecture, real estate and books – about everything except what counts most – you and I."

"Agreed. I've been trying to avoid the subject because I'm ambivalent. I feel I'm in love with you but, having made such a disastrous mistake the first time I'm wary of acting on. A case of 'once bitten, twice shy'."

"I understand, but you can trust me, Coco. I care for you, I would never hurt you, I want to be with you. At the same time, I realize that I am being selfish because my prospects of being around for very long are close to zilch."

"Nonsense. I don't believe that."

Bob resists explaining the seriousness of his condition, fearing Coco may abandon him but in her interest, feels compelled to reveal the worst scenario. "Well, believe it. The cardiologist says the condition causing my breathlessness is progressive — and irreversible. It's likely I've only got a couple, three years on the outside before it does me in."

Coco Takes a moment to absorb what she has been told.. "Bob, that's terrible. I'm so sorry."

"Well, you can imagine, I'm not happy about it either. Of course we're all going to die sometime. But sometime is not the same as receiving a specific death sentence. What can you do? As my father used to say, 'You have to play the hand you're dealt.' Under the circumstances, it doesn't seem to make any sense, you and I living together."

"Maybe not, maybe so. We don't have to decide right now." Coco's remark breaks the tension allowing them to enjoy the excellent cuisine and punctuate it with lighthearted chit-chat. Bob pays the restaurant bill. The snow is still falling as they drive, mesmerized by the quiet and white blanketed way back to the house. By the time they arrive at the house Bob's mood has brightened.

"It's early still, how about a nightcap before you leave?" he proposes. "I can make a fire and we can listen to a little music."

"Yes, that would be lovely," replies Coco.

Bob lights the fire, places snifters of Courvoisier on table in front of the couch, rifles through a pile of CDs, and puts on an old Chet Baker album. Soon they are immersed in Baker's moving trumpet rendition of "My Funny Valentine", at once tender and plaintive. They settle into the couch and he puts his arm around her.

"We've got a lot on our plates, you and I," he says

Coco looks up at him questioningly, then nestles into the crook of his arm. Next, after an eight-bar trumpet intro, Baker is singing the Les Brown lyrics to the old Sammy Fain tune, "That Old Feeling."

> I saw you last night and got that old feeling
>
> When you came in sight I got that old feeling
>
> The moment that you danced by I felt a thrill
>
> And when you caught my eye, my heart stood still
>
> Once again I seemed to feel that old yearning

And I knew the spark of love was still burning –

Bob gently lifts Coco's face to his. They kiss, tentatively at first, then languorously, then

hungrily. They are holding each other tightly and he feels a surge of desire and senses her quickening heartbeat. He stands, pulls her close, hears her sigh as she caresses his cheek with her

fingers. He puts his arm around her waist, leads her slowly into the bedroom, turns off the lights. They undress, slip under the covers, and resume their love making, slowly, deliberately, both sensing a growing urgency. They meld and then, unexpectedly, she experiences a series of small pulsations, intimations of an approaching climax and, responding, he soon reaches orgasm, not the explosive orgasm of youth, but robust and satisfying.

On wakening in the morning Coco crawls on top of him and plants a wet kiss on his lips.

"Good morning, sweetheart."

They roll over on their sides. "How did you sleep?"

"Well. And you, Bob?"

"Yes, wonderfully."

"Last night, Bob, I never expected to – to be able to reach – you know ..."

"A good sign for the future," he suggests.

"I think so – but maybe not in the way *you* mean, not sexually," she replies.

"I'm not sure I understand."

"I think what happened last night, the fact that I was able to, could be my body signaling Coco props herself up on one arm, and looking at Bob, continues. "Now, just as I seem to be unloading some of the baggage that was slowing me down, you've handed me some more. It's heavy, and I'm not at all sure I can carry the load."

"By 'more baggage' you mean my worsening condition?"

"Exactly. If I were to become part of your life now and then, when the chips are down, fail you, be unable to take care of you –

what then? Based on past history, caretaker is a role I'm not good at."

"I understand, and I suppose my feelings for you are blinding me to realities."

Coco replies softly, "Yes, realities, fearful realities."

Bob is reminded of the first line of a poem by the 12th Century Hebrew Poet Yehuda Halevi which his mother, when she was failing, had read to him and which he had committed to memory,

"Tis a fearful thing to love what death can touch." Recalling it now brings tears to his eyes. Not the time to quote it to Coco. Instead, he replies, "Life is hard, my love, but we must persevere."

"Yes, hard," she agrees. Bob reflects, sensing his reply must sound an element of hope. "Nor can we work through something as challenging as this in minutes."

When you are in love, the frailties that cloak your loved one may take on the mantle of virtues and their willingness to reveal those frailties to you, a welcome sign of intimacy and trust. Though Coco's shakiness about her ability to stand on her own worries him, Bob finds her willingness to honestly reveal that to him and to confront it head on, disarming and endearing.

His frown lines dissolve and a smile spreads across his face as he savors the trust she has placed in him in openly confessing her frailties and fears.

"And yet, I do know something rewarding we can do in a few minutes," he says, trying to

lighten the mood

"And, what's that?" asks Coco.

"Rustle up some breakfast."

After she has left, Bob pours himself a second mug of coffee and resumes an earlier conversation with himself. He tells himself that, in spite of his declining physical condition that he and Coco could still find happiness together, that they would still be able to bike, sail, see friends, go to theatre, take trips, that he would be able to take care of her and himself, for a time, at least. They would work it out, somehow. But an inner voice interrupts. "Bob, you're delusional" the voice says. "Sure, maybe you could do those things briefly, but before long you'd likely be shuffling around the house tethered to an oxygen tank, completely dependent on Coco. What kind of a life would that be for her?"

"I know, I know," he answers, "and yet I want so much to be with her. She has been gone less than an hour and already I miss her."

"Bob knows that obsessing over Coco and your deteriorating health is not doing him any good. that he needs to set his mind on something else, to find some absorbing project to work on.

CHAPTER TWENTY-FIVE

The following morning, Bob's friend, Fred Wood is on the phone. Fred is showing noticeable signs of memory loss, calling for the second time in two weeks to check the date on which Bob and the Woods are going together to the Huntington Theatre in Boston to see the revival of Sheridan's 'The Rivals.

"Bob," says Fred, "I think it's a week from this coming Wednesday, but I get a little confused these days."

"Let me check, Fred. Bob is aware that Julie, Fred's wife, is beginning to show signs of memory loss, as well, and may not have been able to remember the date.

"Fred, Glad you checked with me on the date of the play because it's this Wednesday, not next Wednesday. Suppose I pick you two up at 5. That should allow us enough time to drive into Boston, park, get a bite at 'the greasy spoon' next door to the theatre and still make the 7:30 PM curtain."

Bob puts down the receiver and calls Coco.

"Hello, love. I know this is sort of last minute, but I was just reminded that friends and I have tickets for the new production of Sheridan's 'The Rivals' at the Huntington in Boston this Wednesday evening. It's gotten good reviews. Any chance you could make it? I would have called sooner but the date got away from me. If I hadn't gotten a call from my friends, I might have forgotten it completely."

"Bob it does sound like fun. Something has come up – but I don't think it will interfere. I've just received an offer on the house."

"Coco, that's great news."

"Could be, but it's a lowball offer and I've decided to reject it. My broker thinks the buyers will counter with a better offer, but they will be out of town until next Monday. So, if it gets down to phone tag negotiations they probably won't begin until next week. I'll bring my cell phone along, just in case."

CHAPTER TWENTY-SIX

On Friday, a couple of minutes before five o'clock the Woods are standing outside their condo on Ocean Woods Drive when Bob and Coco pull up, but just as they are ready to leave, Fred can't find his eyeglasses and goes back inside in what turns out to be a fruitless search. A couple of minutes, after they are underway, Fred discovers them in his jacket pocket.

On the way to Boston, Coco and the Woods engage in small talk and Coco being able artfully to supply the names of places and people which have slipped from Fred and Julie's memories, captivates them, which pleases Bob no end. Sheridan's comedic fantasy about love, money and misunderstandings is diverting enough, but at the end of the evening Bob begins to feel mildly depressed, as his thoughts return to Coco's reluctance to take a second chance on love and his ebbing health.

CHAPTER TWENTY-SEVEN

Bob is in his office, at the computer, having just put the finishing touches on his monthly column for the Duxbury Schooner.

Facing the probability of Coco being out of his life, his mobility declining and his remaining time foreshortened he decides he must throw himself into some endeavor which will give purpose and meaning to his remaining time. He decides he will write a novel, not of his own life's story but one which will incorporate some of his experiences and the insights he has gained from them. A couple of plot lines come to mind. Better jot them down before he forgets them.

Bob begins typing and has been at it a few minutes when he becomes aware of footsteps behind him and the scent of Chanel 5. Feeling a kiss on his ear, he wheels around.

"Coco!" She puts down the small suitcase she is carrying. He is astonished and overjoyed to see her.

"What a delightful surprise!" Then, catching sight of the suitcase, Bob adds, "Are you planning to stay the night?"

"No, longer than that"

"How long?" he asks, hoping she will, at least, stay through the weekend.

"For the duration, Bob—that's if you'll have me," she replies softly. Suddenly his mouth feels dry, his momentary elation drained by feeling compelled to forewarn her again.

"With the way things are going with me I don't think that's a good plan. You would be boarding a sinking ship— I had been meaning to call you to tell you that, but hadn't gotten up the courage."

"Bob, I know you think you have my best interests at heart, but I must disagree. Remember you telling me that life is a game of cards in which you have to play the hand you are dealt. Remember?" Bob reflects on the pragmatic simile passed on to him by his father.

"Yes, I do, and I believe it, unless you decide it is wiser to fold your hand and withdraw."

"Fold, withdraw? That's not you. You're not one to withdraw from life and, as for myself, I've finally discovered that neither am I. I know it. I feel it. We two are destined to play out this game as partners." Tears well up in Bob's eyes as he is overwhelmed with gratefulness at her words, and he turns quickly back to the computer screen so Coco won't see. He reaches his hand over his shoulder, grasps her fingers and tries to collect himself before speaking.

"We have been dealt a very weak hand, you know. Our adversaries, time and death hold stronger hands and will ultimately defeat us."

Coco sets her jaw. "Well then, so be it, I say, let the game begin. We will play our cards thoughtfully, and caringly, my love, and, our victory - our victory will be in the playing."

ABOUT THE AUTHOR

Dick Rothschild's breadth of experience, as commandant of a war criminal stockade in the South Pacific in World War II, father of four boys, marketer, inventor and entrepreneur, and his loss of a spouse and two sons, have provided him with the insights needed to create this gripping novella.

THE END GAME'S flesh and blood characters, Bob Rosenbaum and Coco Cipriani embody strength of character and sense of humor the author found in family members and close friends.

Though life's demands directed him to other enterprises for many years, Dick Rothschild retained an unquenchable love of writing. It sprouted in columns for the freshman paper at Yale, advertising copy written during his sales and marketing career and finally blossomed on retirement when, after completing a writer's correspondence course, he freelanced articles for a dozen national periodicals including American Health, The Writer and The Saturday Evening Post.

On moving to the South Shore of Massachusetts, Dick took up journalism. His column,

"To Your Health" for The Old Colony chain of newspapers became the basis for his first book, "Your Health & Fitness, simple sensible strategies." A growing interest in the environment then lead him to co-found the hometown volunteer advocacy group, Sustainable Duxbury, and to begin a newspaper column for The Duxbury Clipper titled "Thinking Green."

After writing the column for almost a decade, the idea for the novella, THE END GAME began bubbling up. It took the better part of three years to realize it.

Dick and Olga, his wife of 35 years and their beloved pet, Cat Ballou, live in a seaside mid-century contemporary house which the couple built on Kingston Bay. On a mooring behind the house is their little cat boat, El Gato which has been given a bit part in the novella.

Made in the USA
Middletown, DE
15 November 2019